ASCENDENT PUBLISHING, 1640 Worcester Avenue D613, Framingham, MA 01702
www.ascendentpublishing.com

HARDCOVER EDITION

Grateful acknowledgement is given to w.p. Quigley; cover art, copyright © 2024 by w.p. Quigley.
Foreward by w.p. Quigley, editor, copyright © 2023.

ISBN 978-1-963970-08-1

For all the people who have come apart
and are stitching themselves back together.

S
P
L
I
A Novel

S.N. Humphreys

Foreword

Me and Humphreys go back a-ways. Like, way way back. We *seen* some stuff. We *seen* some things. We *seen* some stuff and things.

Daaaark stuff and things, man.

Nah, not really though – quite the opposite in fact. It just so happens that one of my favorite things about our friendship is always apparent whenever she and I conversate. The mood, the general feeling, the vibe (yuck, I already hate myself for using "vibe" just now) never really seems to have any kind of a heaviness to it, no sense that there's no-go areas of dialogue and communication, and an ever-present feeling of ease when we chat. Every time I talk to Shannon, I find myself in a pleasant state of chilled-the-fuck-out I rarely experience in any other context of my life .

Even when her and I willfully gravitate towards complex subject matter that bear entire chromosomes of apprehension, awkwardness, and dread as part of their DNA, we always go back and forth with a temporary immunity to the pandemic of instant outrage and overreaction – the kind of zero to a hundred decibels level anger - that kicks off from even the most marginal of disagreements.

This plague has destroyed discourse across the planet, so finding someone to talk about and discuss these issues with whom you can be certain the above won't occur is refreshing, an oasis, and something each and every one of us needs, like a good hug or even just a positive word or two. It's something you don't know or can be really aware of just how critical its importance is to your sanity until it's been taken from you, and you don't notice its absence straightaway because it isn't like food, water, or shelter.

There's something about Maslow's Hierarchy of Needs in there somewhere towards the top of that pyramid everyone saw in tenth grade psych class but only took in the colorful triangle aspect of the diagram.

That last part - people losing their minds on each other whenever they feel even the slightest bit challenged or insulted plays out again and again and again on social media when I try to interact with people about the very same shit. Disheartening breaks a person down and pushes one towards and eventually into despair faster than we can adjust, let alone effectually combat or prevent.

And so, when I speak of mental instability, conversational minefields, and how interactions with my friend, colleague, and author S.N. Humphreys are easy-breezy rides on the Low Stress Express, there could no more fortuitous and serendipitous confluence of circumstances for you, dear reader, than holding this taut and sharply written novel, *Splinter*.

The character whose mind you are about live in for the next couple hundred pages or so is most definitely *NOT* rent-free living; her descent into the throes of her condition is harrowing, anxiety-inducing, and frankly frightening at times. I'll never forget the Sunday afternoon not so long ago when three of us at Ascendent individually sat down and set about reading the proto-*Splinter*, the novella *We All Fall Down*: each of us read it entirely that same day, despite our intention "to start it" that afternoon.

We never had a chance. To a person, each of us couldn't put it down once we'd started, and despite its effectiveness in immersing the reader into a psychological house of horrors before any of us could mark any of the exits, we each found that none of us really had *wanted* to find the exits. Instead, we desired instead to follow our guide, the writer of the tale in this case, all the way to the end. Because, and for no other reasons other than these:

It was important, and:

We knew we'd each be okay in the end regardless of how the experience may affect or change us.

Splinter represents a landmark achievement, in my estimation, as one of the most accurate characterizations and depictions of the onset, progression, effects, and eventual triumphs over one of the most misunderstood and difficult pathologies the human mind can suffer – paranoid schizophrenia. Be forewarned; each of the three readers who embarked upon the literary journey the work took us that day felt as if we'd each had a far better understanding of what the havoc this condition can wreak upon the human psyche. But like I said, we all felt like we were in good hands. Our trust in author was unimpeachable.

Because, well...it's honest, it's full of soul and heart, and most importantly, truth.

Kinda like my homegirl Humphreys. Turns out she's *seen* some stuff and things, and its show and tell time.

-w.p. Quigley
November 2023

In a Forest clearing
savage shadow demons dance
to the beams of light reflected
in my interested eyes' glance.

FormS of darkness undulate
indifferent, unaware

to the pounding of the drums
with their arms thrown in the air.

Claws clutch at living light,

(the kind which can't be caught).
My eyes in disbelief gaze on,

my mind recedes in thought.

My emotions seem unreal to me,

like some ephemeral dream...
Mind muddled, gaze glazed,

soul tRapped within this trance,
What does it mean
(if anything)
to watch these demons dance?

F i r s t,

Chapter 1

There are moments of clarity in life that hit you full on, like the proverbial grand piano falling from the sky and landing right smack on your big, fat cartoon head. Mine came in the middle of a panic attack precipitated by the ingestion of two blue microdots. I'd been glued to the couch for what felt like hours, unable to move and unsure of just what I was saying, and what I was only thinking. My heart was racing, and I couldn't see the room anymore, just hazy green soup filled with random hallucinatory flashes of things and people and places I'd never seen or known or been to, when it came.

Well...this is it. It's over now. You've splintered. You're insane, and you aren't ever going to be right again.

I turn my head- it's all I can do now - and look at him. My fiancé, the man I love. He looks strange beside me, oblivious to my impending madness. He's smiling at me, as if to say, "Isn't this a good trip?"

I'm suddenly shocked that I could love somebody so blind and completely clueless. I'm losing my mind right next to you, you moron.

He turns to the television, still smiling. There's a movie on, but I cannot for the life of me tell what it is. We'd already watched *Army of Darkness* but that ended ages ago and we'd started playing another movie. . .it was. . .but *Natural Born Killers* couldn't possibly still be playing, could it?

He turns back and I'm still staring. I haven't moved, couldn't move, and confusion is slowly beginning to register on his face.

I love you. Am I thinking or speaking? I hate you. You're an idiot and I loathe you. I'm crying. I've been crying, but I've only just noticed. His lips are moving. He looks troubled. His lips are moving, and I can't hear what he's saying as my ears have taken the evening off. I think he's asking what I said.

What did I say? Did I just tell him that I hate him? Did I say that? I must have. I laugh, but I'm still crying.

A light goes on. The room's quiet. He's stopped the tape and wants to know what's wrong. I can't close my eyes. What's wrong? Nothing is wrong...I'm just fractured. This is how it's supposed to be. This is how I'm meant to be. This is just exactly what he wanted. I've only just realized that, as well.

He's helping me up, but I don't want him touching me. I still can't see, really, my mind is still awash with talking pictures, people that don't exist trying to help me get through it. The visions trying to talk me down. I'm standing; walking like an invalid, his hand on my elbow directing me to the spare room. I see the world as if through a broken kaleidoscope. Nothing is connected. The bed is there. Do I want a drink? Do I want him to stay, to talk? What do I need?

No, I need quiet. I need to be alone. Silence is all I want. Silence will be what I covet most. For four more years, pure silence will be all I crave.

Just go away. I want to lay here and wait for sleep.

Chapter 2

The next day finds me in bed, trying to still my mind by not moving my body at all. As if you can trick yourself into being ok by playing dead. Quiet... still... and just maybe. Maybe the pieces will glue themselves together.

No? Well, okay. This isn't really a shock. Somewhere in the deep dark back end of knowing, we knew it wouldn't be that easy.

"We" is a strange thing to think of yourself as, I suppose, but I can hear the first coming. She, (it-whatever), is barreling down the hallways of my mind right now, so fast she's kicking up sparks. Fast enough to arrive in a sonic boom, flush with guilt and accusations. Soon there'll be so many they'll blend together and drown me in their collective din, but for now there is only this one. The first voice.

I don't notice anything different about this, this extra voice. Sometimes she sounds so understanding...so friendly.

Get up. Get out of bed already. Go see.

Yeah, okay. I'll go see. I'll go back to his room. There's this dread, though, there's really no other word for it. It's washing over me like a wave. I'm afraid to go in there. I'm afraid to see.

It is horrendously unnerving when your sanctuary is taken away from you. Your private happy place: the place you go to feel like yourself. It is doubly so when anything and everything that has ever passed for one is utterly and irrevocably destroyed.

This room- this room with the bubblegum pink walls and the Christmas lights strung up near the ceiling, with the ratty tweed couch and lime green leather chair; this room with words written on the ceiling in laundry detergent so that they can only be seen in black light. His room - this room once passed for a sanctuary.

This was a place for getting stoned, for fucking on the floor, for dreaming, for laughing. In this room I was a queen, I always had the best seat and I always got to pick the next CD or movie. If I wanted to write, or to be alone, I could. If I wanted to be surrounded by friends, they were already there. This is the room where I'd met Alexandra, with her black eye and her fat lip from her (newly) ex-boyfriend. This was the room in which I'd had 8 orgasms in one hour.

But now...well, what about now? Now it's the room where I had my first bad trip.

That was far more than a bad trip, and you know it.

That voice again, goading me. Okay. Yeah. This is the room where I splintered. There was me before, and me after, and there was not going to be any going back.

Now the events of the evening, (the events in my head, at least), come back to me in a rush. I have no future with this man, first of all. I saw that clearly. It won't stop me from wasting the next five years of my life in trying to prove myself wrong, of course, but I know it will end. In fact, it is already over. Whatever we had, it's dying slowly before me, and there's nothing I can do but watch it die.

Well, that's uplifting.

That's the least of it, this voice seems to have hands of gossamer. Silk appendages massaging it all out of me.

There are worse things than losing a man who will never love you enough, anyway. What's more important?

Well, I seem to be a bit insane. I mean, I'm letting a voice in my head direct my inner monologue.

Am I just a voice, now? It's not like I'm new. Feel me. Don't you know me?

There is a sort of feeling when she speaks, a sort of hazy familiarity, like I've always known her.

Well, that's a relief - I was beginning to think you weren't going to recognize me. Feel it out, you'll get it.

Feel it out? I suppose this is supposed to be my intuition.

Suppose?

Fine. I'll play along. You're intuition. I've intuited the end of this relationship, and the end of my sanity. But intuition has never spoken before - it's just a feeling.

Maybe you just weren't listening hard enough.

Hmmm. Maybe. Who knows? Certainly not me, I'm insane. There's too much going on in here, and I really can't think.

What's going on? There is nobody here but you. The TV is off, as is the radio. No one is even in the house.

She's right, of course, the house is deserted. He must be at work. It's dark and it's silent but - it isn't. It's sort of like my senses are guitar strings, and somebody is strumming away. There is all this static. My head is full of it. Most of it is nothing, but there's an odd word or phrase cutting through.

I feel like a television set to a UHF channel, all fuzz and colored lines and random nonsensical noise. Is this what being insane is like? Is this it?

This is nothing. You're just open. You just wait, you'll see.

I call my mother to pick me up. I want to be alone, but I don't want to sit in this house all day. That room feels like a tomb now. No, like a gaping maw of need, a sentient digestive tract that craves my pain. I left all my things in there, though.

His calico cat follows me. "What are you doing off the bathroom sink, Vyv?" She never leaves that sink. She looks at me with her saucer eyes and then walks away.

I walk down the hall, which suddenly seems foreboding. I'm edgy still, ready to jump at the slightest sound.

"MAGGIE!!!"

It's a booming voice, directly in my right ear. It's a man, deeper and more resonant than any voice I've ever heard. It's not like Intuition, (Oh great, I'm calling that one by name now), at all. It's from outside of me. I swear, it's real. I can feel the air shake with its vibration, can feel the breath on my ear.

Of course, there is nobody here. I run to the pink room and grab my bag. I slam the door shut and prop the TV tray under the handle. I'm shaking. What the fuck? What the fuck is wrong with me?

Now THAT – that is insane.

Thanks a lot for the comment from the peanut gallery. I'm on the floor hugging my knees to my chest saying, "What do you want?" over and over again. It takes me a few minutes to notice. I need to breathe. I move the TV tray and crack the door open. "Who's there?" I know I'm talking to empty space, but I have to convince myself. There's nobody there but the air seems to be giggling at me.

Maybe I'll watch TV until my mother arrives. TV is great, you don't have to think, you just sit back and take in the stimuli, right?

Oh yes, you need more stimuli. The silence isn't talking to you enough.

Here's an idea, Intuition. Why don't you go fuck yourself? I'm not exactly desperately in need of your input right now.

Silence.

Hey, that actually worked.

Chapter 3

Okay, TV. *click* It's on. When did I start doing an inner monologue of everything I do? Stop that. Now.

I think A & E is a little beyond my comprehension skills at the moment, I need something mindless. MTV. Yes. Good. Any music? No, the news.

Madonna is doing something, but I'm not sure what. I can't concentrate. Kurt Loder is looking into the camera when he speaks. Why is he looking at me like that?

He's doing the news; they always look into the camera.

Didn't I ask you kindly to fuck off?

"In other news, our little Maggie has completely lost it. She thinks I'm talking to her right now. She's been a bad little girl, our Mags. We think it may have been the drugs. On the other hand, maybe she's just never been appreciative of all the advantages she's had in life. Maybe she's just wasted it all, and now it's too late. Looks like the loony bin for Maggie. In honor of this momentous occasion, we're going to play a fitting video from the Dr. Demento archives. So here it is, kids, They're Coming To Take Me Away..."

click

What did I tell you, Maggie? Too much, huh?

Oh, shut up.

What exactly is the world coming to when Kurt frickin' Loder tells you you're insane from your TV? Where the hell is my mother? It's only been 5 minutes. Shit. Shit shit shit. This does not look good. In fact, it's looking worse by the second. And I cannot get that voice out of my head. It was too real. This is far beyond my experience or comfort level.

Chapter 4

A car is pulling up. It's my mom. Pull it together, it is time to maintain. Just pretend you're still tripping. She never seems to notice that. Don't want to let mom know we might have lost our mind.

Might have?

Get in the car. Buckle seat belt. Smile. "Thanks, mom."

She has that annoyingly concerned mother look. "Is everything ok?"

"I'm tired. Up late, didn't sleep well,"

think yawn think yawn think....

YAWN

"Mmmmph." That's mother speak for I-know-you-were-up-partying-but-I'm-letting-it-go-for-now.

Terrific. That's what we like to hear. Radio on. Volume up. Staring out the window.

Do you think you'll be better or worse, by the time he leaves?

Fuck. He's leaving. Next week. Off to art school. He'll study movie making, or music. Probably both. I'm not even sure what he's decided. Mostly I don't care. I think it's idiotic. He has no vision, and (I think), no talent. Waste of money. He won't even be here for our anniversary.

Why, you don't seem to think very highly of him. Who cares? Let him go. Let it end when he leaves.

I don't know why. I love him.

Do you?

Yes! Now shut up!

I'm getting agitated, fidgeting in my seat and my mother is eyeing me up. I need to get to my bedroom. Maybe I've not come down all the way. Maybe I'll take a nap and wake up and things will be back to what passes for normal in here. Or, you know, maybe flaming pigs will fly out of my ass and take over the world. I mean, you never really know, do you?

Instead of a restful nap, I have a weird dream. I'm run over by a truck, but I turn into goo. A puddle of gelatinous fat, really, with my bones all whole and poking out. My cousin walks by, and I call out to her to help me, but it's getting dark. I'm not even sure she can understand me. She looks me right in my somehow still whole eyeball and says, "What have you done to yourself *this* time?" I'm dying.

I'm awake, and my heart is pounding.

Aren't death dreams fun? I mean, they can mean sooooo many things, and all the weird little bits are so interesting. I mean, gelatin? What was with the bones? Your cousin - why that cousin? Of all the people who could have walked by....

It's still talking, but I'm in complete denial now. Sleep made things worse. Maybe food? When's the last time I've eaten? Maybe hunger has driven me over the edge? Doubtful, but I probably ought to venture into the kitchen and eat anyhow. I sit up in bed and see her. Mia Wallace is staring at me out of my Pulp Fiction poster. Oh goody. I'm going to smile at her. I mean, it's Uma Thurman, and anyways, I love this poster.

Okay, I've definitely gone far beyond the point of insanity. I'm plotting out how to stay on good terms with my poster, for fuck's sake.

I smile. She smiles back. Wait, what?! I freeze. A voice I might have expected, but that poster's mouth moved. It moved, and I don't know what the hell I'm supposed to do with that. My face is starting to hurt from the smiling. The poster's eyes have taken on this suspicious cast, as if it knows I'm forcing a smile. I have to get the fuck out of here.

"I am absolutely famished," I announce to no one in particular, taking special care not to look Uma in the eyes as I say it. " Better raid the kitchen.

I stretch, "Aaaaah, yeah."

I run from my own room like somebody who's just broken an expensive vase at an intimate charity soiree in a marble floored mansion. You spend your entire life with everyone telling you you're crazy, and then one day it starts to happen, and you think that you really ought to have been more prepared.

I'm grabbing prepackaged, processed sugar. My stepdad loves all those weird little cake-like things with the frosting and the cream inside, and the house is always full of them. I have to get out, and this is fast and portable.

"I'm going for a walk, Ma." I call out as I grab a coat.

"It's January, Maggie," she calls back in that annoyingly concerned tone.

"Yes, Ma. Yes, it is." The door slams behind me. I'm crazy, woman, not stupid.

Chapter 5

Fuck, it's cold.

I have a few dollars. I can walk down to the Citgo and get a big hot chocolate to go with my cakey thing. Nice long quiet walk in the bracing cold. Why not? And if I slip and fall on the ice and crack my head open, maybe everything else will leak out with my brains and blood. Fuck it. That's always been my motto anyhow. Fuck it.

And you've done OH so very well with it, haven't you?

Do you ever run out of things to say?

Do you?

Good point. Go on, then. At least now there's no one else around.

Do you know it's Wednesday? All your friends are in school. You're walking the streets to get hot chocolate and talking to the voices in your head. How have you gotten here, Maggie? Run through it.

Yeah, okay, fine. It was like Jersey all over again. I stopped going to class. I don't cut myself anymore, no. And I suppose it hardly even has to do with boredom and depression now. I spend all of my time with him. I was skipping class too much. I wasn't going to be able to make up the work. I wasn't going to graduate.

So, what did you do?

I freaked out. Told my mom I hadn't been going to class. I told her I was worried. Scared. She called my shrink.

Yes, the one who has you on the Prozac. And how's THAT going?

Don't play games. You know I don't take it. I can't take it. I die inside when I LOOK at the fucking things. I'd rather be depressed than dead. I hate not feeling anything at all. That's why I started cutting in the first place.

The doctors say it's a cry for help. They say cutters hate themselves.

The doctors say a lot of very stupid things. What do doctors know? Something they read in some book? Do they ask? Do they ask the cutters?

They asked you, didn't they?

Yeeeeeeees... but they have to interpret everything. They think everything means something else. You know what, though?

Sometimes things just mean what they mean.

Alright then. You tell me, and I'll believe you, alright? Why? Why did you cut?

Because I got to the point where I couldn't tell what I felt anymore. Everything was the same gray. Everything felt like nothing.

And?

And the cutting felt like pain. Pain is something. It has a name and you know what it is when you feel it. When you feel pain, you know you're alive. You're still there. It all sounds that stupid because it IS that stupid. That doesn't make it any less true, though.

And so they decided I was depressed. Here, have some Prozac. Well, Prozac makes everything feel the same. A different "same", sure. But still the same. Everything isn't gray anymore. Now it's all blue-gray. That's the difference.

So what now?

Obviously, I can't cut anymore, and I don't want to. It was silly and melodramatic, and I've got scars and it scared my mom. She doesn't deserve that, and really, I'm enough trouble without her worrying that I'm suicidal or some other nonsense. Not the Zoloft, not the Prozac. Self medication. That's the way I've gone.

Pot. Pot and acid and beer and whiskey that's your solution?

Well at least I'm having fun. Why not? Millions of people self-medicate. It even works some of the time. It was working out just fine, except for the school thing, but really, I gave up on that 2 years ago.

Did you give up, or did you just feel like you had all the time in the world to catch back up?

Six of one, Half a dozen of the other.

Okay. So your mom calls the shrink. What happened?

I'm not sure what she told her, but the shrink agreed to sign off on me doing home school. Two days a week I have a 4-hour class. That and some homework. That's it. Me and some goth girl. As long as I show up at the teacher's house for my two classes a week, and do my homework, I pass.

Not going to get you into college though, is it?

I already blew the SATs.

An 1170 is not that bad a score.

An 1170 will not get me a scholarship.

Take it again. This time don't stay up all night drinking and then drop a hit of acid an hour before the test.

It won't matter. My GPA is shit. I haven't had an extra-curricular activity in years....no decent college would have me. Who wants a student with a track record of not merely performing below her potential, but out and out defying anyone to teach her anything? What do I tell them, I was too proud to be taught by people I was smarter than? Should I list talking to myself and rolling very serviceable blunts as after school activities?

So, you're really going to marry this guy?

I love him. Yes.

Why?

The woman behind the counter looks at me a little funny, which is odd, because I'm acting completely normal and totally not saying any of this stuff out loud, I think. Of course, I do have a short green mohawk, so that could explain the look.

I get the largest hot chocolate they sell, and head back to a gazebo on the lake near my house.

My mind has been quiet since that last "why", as if the voice, (Intuition), is giving me a chance to think it over. I'm not considering it at all, it frightens me, quite frankly. I'm very attracted to him. Not in a oooh-you're-hot kind of way, but in a stomach churning, I-can-feel-when-he-enters-a-room-without-even-looking sort of way. It's always been like this with us, and it's very much beyond me.

The truth of the matter is, I don't really like him very much at all, if I care to look at it. I feel as though I need him, although I'm not sure just what it is I need him for. The whole situation is very troubling, and my behavior in this relationship is completely unlike me, but the sex is fantastic. Really. I think it's entirely possible that that is all we have. That and a similar taste in movies. I know I won't leave him. I can't. I don't know what it is, but I can't, so I might as well go on deluding myself.

The gazebo is covered, and so the stone bench, while uncomfortably frigid, is completely dry and ice free. I sit, feeling the cold of the stone seep through my trousers, and drink my hot chocolate, looking out at the frozen lake through the steam. If the voice comes back, I can entertain it, as there is nobody around. If it doesn't, I can enjoy the quiet.

If this is all it takes to make me feel content, why am I always so damned miserable? Is this what it's like for homeless people?

Homeless person 1, "How was your day today?"

Homeless person 2, " It was a great day. Nobody tried to set me on fire."

I lied.

You and everyone else. What about?

I don't believe you. I don't entirely believe you, anyway. I do think you hate yourself, or at least you dislike yourself quite a bit. Not because of the cutting, though. You've given up, and you're perfectly willing to throw your life away on this guy. This guy you say you LOVE but you don't actually like, and if that isn't self-sabotage, then what is?

I won't give this up. It's probably stupid, but sometimes it's like it's the only good thing I've ever felt. I cannot just walk away from that.

I know.

Intuition takes a holiday.

I crack the joke in my head, but it's answered with silence. Okay then. I guess I've bought myself some quiet. I should head home, shower, and get ready. He'll be off work soon. We're going to try to squeeze in every last minute together before he has to go. I almost wish he was already off. I don't want him to leave knowing I'm going insane. He'll blame his leaving. That or he'll fuck around on me. One or the other.

Anyway, it's all meaningless. The next week is meaningless. Intuition comes and goes, probing, questioning, accusing. We spend our last week together in a riotous fit of fucking and smoking. He knows something is wrong, that much I can tell, but he probably thinks that I'm sad that he's leaving. And he's right. I am sad. I'm not sad because I'll miss him, (though I will, I'll miss him like I've never missed anyone before), but because everything is ending. He doesn't know it, but soon I won't love him anymore, and I'll never be able to explain.

The timing is wrong, my mind is slipping away, but so is this feeling for him, and I'll never be able to make him see the difference.

Once he's gone, I stop caring. Everyone knows I'm not right.

Everyone thinks I'm depressed.

You have a history of depression.

Depression doesn't talk to you. Depression doesn't keep you up all night with its jabbering. This is something else.

Tell someone.

Tell them what? There's a new voice in my head? I can't sleep.

People suddenly make me nervous? I'm afraid they can hear what I'm thinking? I'm afraid I can feel what they're feeling? Do you know what they do to people who say these things? They lock them up.

Maybe you ought to be.

Maybe. Probably. It doesn't sound like much fun though.

Maybe they're right. Maybe I'm just depressed that he's gone. It's winter, I've never gotten the hang of all the dark and cold. Maybe I'm just extra depressed, and when summer rolls around, and I'm back with him, you'll go away.

Hmph.

Chapter 6

Fuck it. My neighbor, Karen is home. I think she's sucking up my soul whenever I'm around her, but she's got good weed, and she'll smoke me up.

I know it's a mistake the second I walk in the door. Everything is off. My guard is up, like I'm expecting something, but I don't know what. She's laughing, smiling, all hey-sit-down-while-I-roll-one. Her son comes in. Her expression darkens. She's asking if he's cleaned up after the dogs. He's looking at me - it seems like years ago.

I used to babysit Aaron. After a while it became "tutoring" meaning I'd help him with his homework. He never really needed help, just someone to make sure he got it done. When he couldn't concentrate,

I'd take him in the family room.

There were huge couches on either side of the room, flanking the TV. "Okay, Aaron," I'd say, "We'll be like wrestlers - for ten minutes. Then you HAVE to do your homework." I'd stand in the middle of the room and wait. He'd eye me up then run at me. I'd grab him, lift him above my head, then body slam him on one of the couches. That's it. Ten minutes, one couch to the other. After ten minutes I'd say, "Okay, time's up. Homework time."

He'd go to the kitchen, sit at the table, and 20 minutes later he was done. He might ask me a math question, and I'd help him work it out, but that was it. All this kid needed was some attention, just ten minutes of being a kid, and he was fine. I don't even know what made me think of wrestling. I just thought he needed to let off some steam.

A week after that first time with the couches, he came running into the kitchen right after we'd smoked a joint. His mom told him it was adult time, she didn't want him on her lap. He ran right past her. He climbed on me. He gave me a hug and told me he loved me, and he was going to bed.

It's only been a year, but he seems so much older.

"Hey Aaron, how's it going?" I'm searching his eyes, but I don't know what I'm looking for.

"Hi Maggie, long time no see." He won't look at me, not directly. I know I've let him down. I should've stayed around more, kept tutoring him, but I'd found a boyfriend and was too wrapped up in my own life. I hate myself right now.

He needed his mother.

He needed someone to give a fuck. And I do. But it's too late now. All I did was give him false hope and then disappear when he got used to me. I probably just fucked him up worse. Anyway, who the fuck am I? I shouldn't have gotten involved if I wasn't going to BE there.

You aren't his mother.

No, but I've hurt him as well.

He's leaving now. I'm staring at the back of his head projecting at him. I'm sorry Aaron. I'm sorry I'm not older or better. I'm sorry I couldn't do more. No, I'm sorry I didn't do more. But he's already gone.

She's lit the joint and I'm hitting it. Right away I can tell THAT isn't right either. I'm drowning, but not in a good way. The air feels thick and I want to cry. I feel weak. She's smiling at me like some sick succubus demon spawn freak, and the weaker I feel, the more she smiles. She's babbling about her father, about how he didn't pay her car insurance. The words are all running together. *This is what people mean when they talk about psychic vampires.*

The air is thick and purple and I can feel reality slipping through my fingers. Fuck. I'm nodding my head. This seems like an appropriate response, as her grin is widening. She's all teeth and cheekbones, now, she's a shark...a death mask. I want to scream. I want to cry, I want to hide under the covers like a child.

What the fuck is happening to me, anyway?

There is this spot of coldness in my elbows, and at the base of my spine. It grows colder - it builds. It shoots up my arms and spine and congregates in my neck. My head snaps back and forth, five times. What the fuck?

"Are you cold?" she asks. She looks concerned.

"Yeah, actually, I think I just caught a chill." I'm sweating, actually, the room is really warm, but I just spasmed and twitched, and I think this is my out. "I have been feeling a bit off, think I'll go lie down. Wouldn't want to get you sick."

"Drink some orange juice." She nods at me sagely.

"Yeah, thanks. Hey, see you soon, alright?"

"Feel better, Maggie."

Chapter 7

Feel better, Maggie.

If I'm so crazy, why do we always seem to have relatively reasonable conversations?

You aren't crazy yet.

Yet? Thanks for the vote of confidence. You know, I don't actually believe you are intuition, right? What are you, if I'm not crazy... yet.

Does it matter? There will be others soon. Very soon. Before you know it, you'll MISS this... this feeling. The relative quiet. The relative sanity.

Everything is relative, I suppose.

I call Alexandra. I'm not entirely sure why. I haven't wanted to be around anyone lately. I don't really feel comfortable going slowly insane in front of people, especially not people I know. But for some reason, when I'm with Alex, I'm almost comfortable.

She picks me up. We're driving, and she's telling me about her boyfriend. He's been acting strange.

I'm trying to listen, I really am.

I'm trying to keep up. She stops talking. She's looking at me. Has she noticed yet?

"Fuck it, Mags. I've got a bottle of Jack Daniels at home. A small one. Let's go to the truck stop and pick up some trucker speed and just get fucked up."

I'm laughing. "I've got five on the trucker speed."

And we're off.

We get four of the little foil packets. They have two pills, a single dose, in each of them. We're in Alexandra's room now, and she's crushing them up on a CD case. In a few years, people will be dying from ephedra in diet pills, but nobody knows that now. I'm walking over to her CDs, the bottle of Jack in my hands.

"Janis?" I ask, knowing the answer already.

"Fuck yeah!" She's cutting the dose into four lines. "Do it."

I put the CD in as she does her lines. I hand her the bottle with one hand as she hands me the CD case with the other. We're using a cut McDonalds straw.

"Oooooh, look at this," I say while she hits the bottle, "suddenly too good for a rolled-up bill, are we?"

She sticks her tongue out at me as I sit and take the straw. One line per nostril. The trucker speed hits immediately when snorted, but the whiskey is the secret ingredient. She passes me the bottle. A few shots of this turns the trucker speed almost trippy. Our four little packets are more than enough to get us through an evening.

Janis is wailing, "Take another little piece of my heart now baby...." I'm laughing at something Alex just said. I almost feel normal. Ah, fuck it.

"I think I'm losing my mind."

Alexandra looks at me, then busts out laughing. "I think you lost it ages ago."

"I'm completely serious, Alexandra. I haven't been right for weeks, and I think I'm going to keep getting worse."

She's eyeing me up again, trying to gauge my sincerity. "What do you mean by 'haven't been right', exactly. You're just depressed because you miss. . ."

"It's not just that. It started before he left, and it really hasn't got fuck-all to do with him, to tell you the truth. I've been talking to myself lately. Not like, 'Hey, dumbass, you locked your keys in the car' kind of talk...but actual conversations."

Her face has done that conversion from "ha-ha" to "hmmmmm". This is Alex 'private investigator' expression. Her I'm-going-to-figure-this-shit-out-NOW look.

"Do the conversations make sense?"

Sigh. "For the most part, so far. But I don't think they will much longer. I've been thinking really strange things lately."

"Strange how?"

Deep breath, Mags. I've barely even acknowledged these thoughts yet. They scare the crap out of me.

"I keep getting the feeling that everyone can hear my thoughts - and that I can hear their thoughts as well. I feel out of tune. Like someone broke off the volume knob trying to turn it up as high as it would go and set the radio to where it's picking up two different stations. It's all a lot of gibberish, but it's drowning me out and I can't think. I don't know how else to explain it."

"Okay. Well, fuck it. You'll be fine."

"I'll be fine?"

"Yeah. Just tell me when you're going crazy. It's not like you're the first person to go nuts, right? Besides, it'll prepare us for when I lose my mind."

She's completely serious. She's basically right, as well. It's not like I have a choice in the matter. If I'm going to go insane, I can't stop it. Somehow, this all helps.

"Eh, fuck it. It's not like I was ever all that sane to begin with."

"That's the spirit," she says, passing me the bottle.

Chapter 8

On my own, my brave-face-mask crumbles. I'm lying on my bed, staring at the ceiling, because it hasn't got any eyes. At least not so far. And as long as I'm looking at something without eyes, I can pretend my posters aren't talking to me. I mean, I know they aren't actually talking to me. I know this. But - I can hear them. These voices that don't come from outside. They don't sound like me and they seem to come from outside...

It's one thing to know that these things aren't real; that your mind is playing tricks on you. It's all very well and good. But they go on existing no matter how much you assure them that they, in fact, aren't possible. And they FEEL real. They cut into you as surely as a surgeon's scalpel. They find the soft squishy parts, and they stick their claws right in and dig and tear and root around for the good stuff. You get the feeling that it doesn't matter if they're real or not. They're real enough, and they're hungry. They want your pain, and they know how to get it.

You would be forgiven for wondering why I wouldn't try to get help at this point. At any point. The absolute surety that the worst thing that could ever happen to me, would be for people to *know*. My mother, my shrink, the neighbors. No one is to be trusted with the state of my brain. It all feels like some vast punishment. I'm not sure what I've done to deserve it, but there would be nothing worse than everyone knowing.

Paranoia is insidious. It reaches its claws right down into the base of your being and pulls your strings. You don't even realize how much of what you're doing stems from the delusions it has implanted in your thoughts.

If there is one thing I get from my mother, it's what I call the last-act-of-defiance-attitude. It is ostensibly stupid and pointless. It's rooted in pride, which is why it is generally stupid and pointless. But it's something to cling wildly to in desperate, hopeless situations. What it REALLY is, is a power play by the powerless. A forceful outpouring of free will in the face of hopelessness. It's, basically, saying to the world, " I know what I'm about to do/say is wrong, and will only cause me trouble, but it'll prove YOU wrong, so I'm going to do it anyway, consequences be damned, because I fucking can." and then sticking your fingers in your ears and razzing at the universe.

Pretty much everything I did from this time on was a last act of defiance towards the voices. Simply because they wouldn't shut up, and I couldn't make them. I'd already lost, you see. My only recourse was to be disagreeable, even when the voices were trying to help me.

Fuck you voices! Fuck you very much.

I think, in going insane, it helps to be slightly pig-headed and crazy at the outset. What I mean is, being naturally irrational in my reactions to things probably helped me keep myself. I am a

creature of disorder and chaos. One look at my bedroom or my purse can attest to this fact.

When I was in sixth grade, my teacher nominated me to go into the gifted and talented program in junior high. The junior high G&T teacher came to interview me. My teacher brought her in in the middle of class.

"This is Mrs. B, Maggie. Open your desk, please, and show it to her."

Now, we had the sort of desks with a hinged lid. You put your books and pens and stuff inside, and the wooden part of the desk shut down over them. Except, of course, mine didn't shut. I couldn't manage to squeeze all my crap in there, so there was about an inch and a half of space there. The writing surface of my desk was actually angled away from me, unless I rested my elbows on it. I couldn't put a pen down, because it would roll right off, so I chewed them instead.

"Why, who is she?" I asked, "Is she with the health department?"

My teacher rolled her eyes at me. "Nevermind who she is, just do it."

I looked at the pregnant woman who was patiently waiting to view the contents of my desk. "I'm sorry," I said, as I lifted the lid.

"Ah," she said. That was it, just "Ah."

There were six lunches in there....some of them were so old, I was afraid to touch them. Paper everywhere. Lots of notes to my friends.

Five books I was currently reading which had nothing to do with school. Mark Twain, Steven King, and a few Hardy Boys mysteries. Some Happy Meal Toys. A Walkman and five or six cassettes. Eraser bits and the broken off metal clip from a pen that I used to break off eraser bits to throw at people when I was bored. I was bored a LOT, so there were a LOT of eraser bits.

"I'm really sorry if that frightened you." I felt bad because she was very pregnant, and it really smelled kind of awful in there.

"Do you know, " she said, as if commenting about the weather, "historically, most geniuses are either compulsively neat or disgusting slobs?"

"Thank you, Maggie." My teacher said, and then they stepped outside to speak privately.

But that was eons ago. Well, five years, really, but it seemed like eons.

Now I was lying on my bed, sweating and shivering and trying desperately not to respond to the voices mocking me.

Did you know, historically, a high percentage of geniuses go mad?

Well, seeing as I'm not actually a genius, I must be safe, right? No madness here. Ha ha. I'm grinding my teeth and hugging myself. They're bound to go away sooner or later - aren't they?

Oh, I don't know - it's rather nice here. I think I'd like to stay a bit. What's your favorite poem, Maggie?

"Twas brillig and the slithy toves did gyre and gimble in the wabe-"

All mimsy were the borogoves and the mome raths outgrabe.

Gibberish. Utter nonsense.

Well-crafted gibberish. They feel like real words. The whole poem is made-up words, but it still tells a story you can follow. It's fucking genius.

It's madness, Maggie. Did you fall down the rabbit hole? Have you gone through the looking glass?

Stop answering!! Why am I answering? Why am I debating poetry with a voice in my head?

Because you're mad, Maggie. It's okay though. We're all mad here.

I see something moving out of the corner of my eye.

Don'tlookdon'tlookdon'tlookdon't

Yes, don't look, Mags!

I look. There's a shadow in the corner. I cast my eyes around the room trying to figure out what's making it. There's nothing. It's moving. It MOVES. Its head turns toward me. It has shadow horns and its tail moves languidly. It looks at me with piercing red eyes.

My stomach turns over on itself. What the fuck is happening to me?

It smiles at me. I cannot see this so much as feel it. It's only a shadow, I tell myself, but shadows are just darkness, and this is blackness. Complete absence of light. I feel sick. Its smile widens for a second, and then he's off. He's running. He circles the room. I lose sight of him, but I can feel those red eyes burning through me. What does he want?

He's only watching you, Maggie.

"WHY?" I say that out loud, probably yell it, and I'm very thankful nobody is at home but me.

Maybe he's your guardian, keeping an eye on you. You didn't think you'd have an angel, did you?

I don't even believe in that crap.

You don't have to believe things for them to be real, you know.

Go to hell.

How do you know I'm not there? How do you know YOU aren't?

Oh goody. An existential discourse with the made-up voices in my head. Yippee. If I'd known you were coming I'd have baked a cake, baked a cake! I'm singing it in my head. I laugh out loud. It's more of a cackle.

There you go, embrace the madness.

"Fucking fuck shit!" I'm yelling again. I don't want this.

Chapter 9

I put on a CD. I'm going to drown this shit out. Nine Inch Nails - *The Downward Spiral.*

Great choice for going mad.

It's new, it's just come out. It's angry and it's Trent and I love it. I already know all the words. I turn it up louder. I'm on my bed, jumping, screaming along. Uma is staring, so are Bruce Lee and Travis Bickle and Janis Joplin. I can feel them all biting their tongues, waiting to see how this plays out. Except of course, they haven't tongues to bite. I have to stop thinking like they're real. I KNOW they aren't. But for some reason, my mind skips around this knowledge.

I'm tired of this soup I'm swimming in. The world around me has this sense of fictitiousness - it's disconcerting. Reality feels made up. The world inside is more real than the walls of my room. I'm slamming my hands against the wall, trying to feel it. It's there but it's like I'm not. I'm somewhere else, the fractured place. I'm afraid, and angry at my fear.

Uma's right, this is a great CD to go mad to. I'm laughing again, but it's just anger. I suddenly feel very cheated. Somebody is getting the short, shitty end of the stick, and I'm quite sure it's me.

You always knew this was coming, didn't you?

I've torn Uma down the middle. Half the poster is still hanging on my wall.

"Anybody else got anything insightful to add to the fucking conversation?!" I'm screaming at my walls. "Hmmm? Because I'm not really in the mood for fucking company."

It's quiet. I feel like an ass, but it's quiet. I crumple up the poster in my hand, and tear the other half off the wall. I'm screaming at no one. I'm still standing on the bed, sort of bouncing. I throw the crumpled bits of Uma on the floor. I jack up my CD player as loud as it will go.

"All the pigs are all lined up, I give you all that you want, take the skin and peel it back, now doesn't it make you feel better?"

Yes, Trent's great for the rage and insanity. How does one deal with going insane? I guess you climb right inside and own it. What else can you do? At least for today, it's mine.

"I'm stuck in this dream. It's changing me. I am becoming." I'm laughing. I wonder how many song writers have gone insane. I mean, completely and utterly balls to the wall bonkers. Is it just that the insane can read their own situation into anything they hear, or do these people have some special insight into the human psyche?

I don't want this CD to end. I'm afraid of the quiet. I'm afraid I'll ruin it completely. It won't be the voices - it'll be me. I'll break the seal. As much as I hate their existence in the first place, I'm filled with questions. Questions for whom, I'm not sure.

The music is like electricity through me. I can feel it. I feel everything lately. As though my sense of empathy has increased a thousand-fold. Usually it's just overwhelming. Right now it feels good. It's all going through me, and I can feel it.

"You didn't hurt me-nothing can hurt me-you didn't hurt me-nothing can stop me now."

The songs are directing my thoughts, really. I'm picking up on lines and running with them, I'm interpreting my madness through these lyrics. But they fit so well, it's hard not to feel it's the other way around.

"my new consciousness."

I know the delusions are only getting stronger. They'll take over completely soon. I cannot avoid this. I always thought that crazy people didn't know they were crazy, but I know it won't be that way for me.

I'll still be in here, watching myself lose control, reacting to delusions I know aren't true, and completely unable to stop myself. I should be afraid, but I'm comforted. I'll lose all control, but I'll still exist. I'll be in there, waiting.

Chapter 10

By the time spring comes, I'm barely functioning. Everyone still seems to think I'm just depressed, though. I've retreated to my cell. I only scream at the voices silently, in my head, most of the time. I don't want help. I want to do this myself. I know it's a stupid thing to think; I don't care. This is my vision quest, this is my test, my trial. This is a battle for me to win or lose on my own.

I don't really speak anymore, except a bit to Alexandra. And to him, on the phone. I babble about missing him, I tell him I'm insane, and he seems undisturbed. He doesn't believe me. He'll know soon enough. Graduation is coming. The next day, my parents will drop me and everything I own off at the apartment we picked out together, a day's drive away. Then he'll be fucked too.

None of this disturbs me. I've warned him repeatedly. He laughs. He thinks it's ok and that he's crazy too. He doesn't know what crazy is. I don't know what crazy is. Every day I get worse, every day I have a new definition for crazy. The days are just slivers of consciousness bundled together haphazardly. What happened a week ago might have been this morning. It's all jumbled like the pieces of a broken plate brushed into a dustpan.

He tells me I'll feel better when I'm with him again. I try to tell him I won't. I'll only go on getting worse until I can't get any worse. Then, I figure my chances are about 50/50. Either I stay insane, or I start to get better. No telling which, really. He's quiet. I've hurt his feelings by saying his presence won't heal me, or something. As if he's Jesus Christ or some shit. I put the phone down. None of it really matters.

Moving in with him is a huge mistake. I know his as soon as I see him again. He's grown a goatee and he looks like a goddamned Disney villain. I feel a wave of revulsion wash over me. I want to turn around and climb back into my step dad's pick up and leave dollar-store Jafar and this nightmare world behind, but I say nothing. My parents get back in their truck and start the drive back home.

I am three hundred miles from home. Three hundred miles from anyone and anything else I know. He works, he goes to school. I stare for hours at the shadows on the wall, dancing like flames. There are so many voices that Intuition is almost drowned out now. I am never alone. The shadow demons peep in the windows, indistinct ghosts wander the apartment, going about their daily chores.

I spend each second of everyday mourning. I mourn the loss of my mind; I mourn the death of our love. I cannot love anyone in this state. I can feel it all slipping through my hands and out of my soul, as if I am the lid of some great cosmic toilet. Watching helplessly as it all gets flushed away.

When I walk the streets, people stare. I've got bright pink hair and that's probably why, but in my mind, they can see the giant neon question mark suspended above my head at all times, advertising the fact that nothing makes sense anymore. Look at me, the amazing question girl! She never knows what the hell is going on.

The TV tells me to follow the signs, crack the code, so I rarely turn it on, but I follow the signs all the same. And they're everywhere. Up the walls, on the doors, hidden in the folds of my blanket.

Sometimes I laugh at nothing. Mostly I cry. I cry for the quiet that used to exist. I cry because I hate him. I cry for Janis warbling in the other room. I cry for myself.

My mother calls almost every day at first. It angers me. It angers me because I can't think, and it takes all of my willpower to sound even remotely sane. It is important I sound sane, that I don't let on to her that I am a seething mass of psychosis. I'm not sure why, exactly, but it is Important. I finally snap at her, tell her to stop bothering me so much. She only calls once a week. This gives me more time to concentrate on the Big Mystery.

He doesn't speak to me anymore, which is fine as I can't grasp the meanings. Words trickle in my ears and dance around in weird formations, twisting and turning and disintegrating into dust. What good are they? What good is he? Sitting

there, refusing to look at me, ignoring my laughter and tears and whispered conversations with no one. He can't help me, or he won't. He's just a voyeur. Witness to my decline, powerless and fucking pointless.

He leaves again, I don't care where he's gone. I put on music and decide to make some ramen. I will eat, that's a thing people do and I'm still a person, even though I can't remember when I last ate. I sit on the couch and shovel the buttered, cheesy noodles into my mouth. I'm ravenous. I start to cough. Suddenly my noodles reappear, wet sick on my plate.

EAT IT.

This voice is new, it's booming, commanding, my whole body resonates like a gong being struck. I'm staring at a plate of vomit and wondering why this is happening.

EAT IT. DO NOT MOVE UNTIL YOU EAT IT.

Now, I spend a lot of time doing what the voices tell me. I look for the signs, I keep my secrets. But this is too much. I am not going to eat a plate of sick. I shake, the chewed-up noodles dance in their sick bath.

EAT IT.

The fuck I will. I walk to the kitchen, the walls shimmering and shaking in the wake of the voice, and I dump it all in the bin. I rinse the plate, still shaking. I feel like I've defied a god. I feel it's eyes on me, all full of righteous anger at my defiance. I wash the other random dishes in the sink, waiting for it to pass, this feeling, but it escalates. I turn around and the door to my room is glowing blue and bright. I walk slowly towards it, the trepidation building up like a wave about to crest.

I knock even though no one is in there. Why am I knocking on the door to an empty room? I feel like I'm in trouble. I disobeyed and something is mad at me. I'm not welcome here. The air feels heavy with judgment. I have been tried and sentenced. What the fuck do I do? What fresh hell am I in for now? I feel as if a door has closed on me. It's cold and I'm alone. I'm being shunned, by what, exactly, I have no clue.

The phone is ringing. When did that start? *Please be Alexandra.*

It's Alex. I feel a chorus of angels, voices rising, inside my mind. Finally someone who can distract me from all… this. We talk about her fiancé. It sounds like he's more into his dildo than he is into her. She's worried that she isn't enough for him. What if he's gay?

I try to reassure her. He's just experimenting and has discovered his prostate, probably. I tell her about my current hallucination, a shadow person staring at me through the kitchen window. I do not mention the voice, and the vomit. We talk for hours about everything and nothing. It's the only real conversation I'll have for weeks.

Chapter 11

He brings home a friend, all sandy haired and big grinned. I'm immediately repulsed by him. They have beer and sit down to play video games. I can feel their eyes on me. How long can I sit here silently and not be an embarrassment? I want to disappear into the couch. He has the eyes of a date rapist. I'm not even sure what that means but I'm suddenly overwhelmed by the truth of it.

I mumble something about being tired and force myself to walk slowly to the bedroom. I close the door behind me and lean against it. I look around and the walls are covered in glowing blue cartoon penises.

This is new. I can hear them laughing and chatting in the other room, oblivious to this new level of fuckery my brain has foist upon me. I decide I'm going to ignore it. It's not real. None of this shit is real. I climb into bed. Oh good, they're on the ceiling too.

I shut my eyes and try to clear my mind. It's like someone's turned on 4 radios, each one set in between two different stations. I decide to stare at the penises. They're all different sizes, some pointed up, some pointed down, all partially erect. Each one gives off a faint blue glow, like strings of phallic fairy lights. I bask in the glow and lay back with my hands under my head, taking in this nonsense like a stargazer on a clear night.

Freud would have a field day with this.

Yeah, well, Freud wanted to screw his mom.

I shut my eyes again and roll over, waiting for sleep to come. At least the penises aren't talking. Or moving. I don't think I could handle it if they were wriggling around, or spinning. Or bobbing around like they were laughing at some secret joke. I crack an eye open to make sure they aren't moving.

Sleep finally comes, but my dreams are weirder than glowing penises. From the waist down, I'm a motorcycle. I can feel my engine rev, my wheels spin. The world is green and glowing, I speed around, stopping to chat with other cycle people, my engine idling. I feel as though I've evolved somehow. I wake up and the blanket is swirled all around me, as if I'd been revolving on the bed on my side. It's still dark and the penises are gone. I'm alone.

I light a cigarette and sit down on the floor in front of the television. The news is on, and a man with too many lines on his forehead is reading it. I try to listen, to pick up the thread of what he's saying but it eludes me. My childhood blanket is tacked up over the window to stop the glare. It's Winne the Pooh, and the hundred-acre wood. In the folds and creases I can make out arrows and strange glyphs.

"It is of vital importance that Maggie figures out what these strange symbols mean."

It's the newscaster.
I look back at the television.

"Do you understand what's at stake, Maggie? Everything. Absolutely everything."

I stare at the blanket again. The symbols appear and then fade away.

They seem meaningless. My cigarette burns down to the filter and snaps me out of my stupor. I drop it in the ashtray and stare some more. Now the symbols are gone. I can't see anything but Pooh bear and Piglet and trees. I start to cry. Somehow, I've failed at this too. The sniffles turn to sobs. Why am I so useless?

"Why are you crying?" He's here. I'd forgotten he was there, on the couch, watching the news. I don't answer. I can't answer. It's all too much.

"WHY are you crying?!" He is inches away from my face now. Suddenly I'm on my back, his hands around my neck. "Why are you crying? WHY ARE YOU CRYING?"

I feel my body go as numb as my mind as he shouts and chokes me. Why am I crying? Is it because I can't make sense of anything, even my own delusions? Is it because I'm afraid I'll be like this forever? Is it because my fiancé is choking me? My whole body feels like pins and needles. He gets up, mumbles something, then walks out the front door. I wiggle my fingers and look back at the blanket. The symbols slowly return.

When he returns, we go out to a diner for dinner. I order a mid-rare cheeseburger, eyes scanning the room. I feel people stare, but maybe that's just in my mind. My stomach grumbles and turns on itself, I cannot remember the last thing I ate. I begin to feel excited at the thought of food. The smells all around are overwhelming. Knives and forks scrape against plates and I shiver and twitch at the sound of it.

Our food arrives, and I attack my burger like a starved animal, moaning quietly as I eat, juice running down my face. Now people *are* starting to stare. An older lady looks at me in distaste, and I growl at her, teeth bared and mouth full. He hisses at me to stop. I'm feeling manic but I dutifully return my attention to my food. How many days has it been since I last remembered to eat? He doesn't take me out for food again.

Chapter 12

I get a job at a local pizzeria. The old man who runs it takes me into the kitchen to show me how to make a pizza. He pulls a couple of balls of dough out of the fridge and unwraps one, flattening it out on the wooden table. Then he starts turning it over his fist, stretching it out slowly, all the while explaining what he's doing. Now it's my turn. The dough is cold and soft and oily. I push it flat, stretch it a bit then start turning it round over my fist.

It takes me a bit longer than he'd like, but I eventually get the dough stretched out properly. Next he shows me how much sauce to add, how to spread it with the back of the ladle. A few minutes later, I'm putting my first pizza in the oven. I feel almost human.

I make pizza for hours. The voices are silent. Maybe a job will do me some good. Perhaps I've just got too much time on my hands to let my brain run wild.

I leave my first shift and it's pouring rain. I start walking home. It is dark and the rain is cold. People slow down to beep and laugh at me. A car finally stops, a college aged boy asks me if I need a ride. I get in the car and he turns on the heat and I give him directions to my house. It's only a few blocks away now, but he drives me anyway. I tell him about my day making pizzas and he laughs as he pulls up to my door.

"Get yourself an umbrella, Maggie, or at least a raincoat." I thank him for the ride and run inside out of the rain, peeling my wet clothes off as soon as the door shuts behind me.

I work three full shifts before they stop scheduling me. They tell me they hired too many people, but I know the truth. They know I'm a monster and they don't want me there. One too many out loud conversations with myself, caught one too many times staring off into space. I'm surprised it lasted as long as it did. I'm surprised any of this did.

I made a work friend in the three shifts I work, but after another week or two, he stops contacting me. The truth is, my illness is too apparent. No one wants to be around me, which is fine, because I don't want to be around anyone either. I make them almost as uncomfortable as they make me. My boss knows it, my friends back home know it. I am tainted.

Chapter 13

It's April. He gives up on school, and we move back home. Rent a U-Haul, pack up everything and go. An eight-hour ride of complete silence except the radio. Alexandra and her boyfriend come over the night we get back. There is beer and microdots and pot and a whole bunch of shit I don't need.

But I take some anyway. Soon I'm off, even further and deeper into my own world than before. It's a good trip, I'm not complaining. The voices are quiet. People are talking, I'm laughing. I feel like I'm in a comic book, I'm Tank Girl. It's a party. I look over at Alex and I see Janis Joplin. There are flowers in her wild hair, and when she smiles at me, it's Janis's lazy grin. Hours pass. Everyone comes down but me. I'm riding my tank through a kaleidoscope of colors. I don't sleep. Who needs sleep?

My mom arrives to help unpack the U-Haul. I'm wearing yesterday's clothes. My boots feel heavy. I march outside in an exaggerated stride, waving hello.

Clomp. Clomp. Clomp. I'm laughing. I haven't felt this good in ages. My mother is speaking to me through a hazy soup of fog. Brain fog. Pea soup. Pea brain foggy soup. She bundles me into the car.

I'm not laughing now. Words push through the ooze. Emergency Room. There appears to be some sort of emergency. I lift my foot to feel the weight of my boot again. It's oddly comforting.

I'm in a room now, a stark white room with a woman speaking gently.

Her words don't penetrate. Beyond her I can see the desert, and my tank. I want to climb inside it and take it out for a spin. I think the woman leaves. It's so peaceful here.

The woman is back, and I can hear her now. She's asking me questions, what's my name, what day is it, what did I take. I'm in the hospital. She's a nurse. The fog has subsided as much as it ever does. I answer her the best I can. I sign the papers to admit myself into the hospital. She tells me I've been here four hours. They're going to find me a bed. It'll just be a few days, just to make sure I'm okay. I do what I'm told. I always do what I'm told. It seems to generally work out better than doing what the voices tell me.

They find me a bed at a different hospital. I have to go by ambulance. I climb in. He's looking at me. He looks so tired. Imagine being that tired when you haven't done a goddamned thing. I'm glad when the doors shut, and I can't see him any longer. I'm afraid but relieved. This is all inevitable. I should have done this a year ago.

Now everyone will know you're crazy.

They already do. I mean, it's hardly a secret, is it? Everyone who looks at me knows. I've been shouting it into the ether with every fiber of my being for as long as I can remember.

The hospital is dim and quiet. They take me into a tiled room and tell me to get in the bath. They take my boots and my shorts and top and bring me back hospital clothes. I'm told my mother can bring me things to wear tomorrow.

I've missed dinner but the nurse will try to find me a sandwich. I shower in the quiet by myself. I dry off and put on a hospital gown and socks with the grippy soles.

I'm shown the community room. There's a TV and couches at one end, and tables and plastic chairs at the other. People are sitting around, there's a televangelist on the screen. Everyone looks so old. That's because it's after curfew. All the under-eighteens in their rooms. The nurse shows me to my room. There is a girl sitting on one of the beds. The other bed is mine.

"Here is your menu to fill out for tomorrow. Just mark off which of the options you want, and I'll take it down to the kitchen. Wake up is at 6. You will have your weight taken then sit outside the doctor's office and wait to be called in. There will be coffee and orange juice you can have while you wait. Breakfast is at eight in the community room."

I fill out the menu while my roommate complains loudly to the nurse. I hand back my menu.

The nurse leaves.

“They’re going to weigh you because you’re so skinny.” My roommate isn’t looking at me, but she’s talking to me. “Just don’t get in my way and we’ll be fine.”

I turn off the lamp next to my bed and go to sleep. I dream that I am inside out, all my organs are on the outside. Everyone can see the squishy pink parts of me. My heart beats visibly like a jackhammer, my lungs rise and fall in quick, Sallow breaths. I leave sticky wet footprints when I walk. I wake up to a sharp rap on the door and another nurse’s voice. Time to get up and see the psychiatrist.

The word ‘schizophrenia’ is spoken. It hangs there in the air, mocking me.

The doctor prescribes an antipsychotic which I take every morning (after I’ve been weighed) with some orange juice. Then I have a coffee and sit in the hallway waiting to talk to him.

I stare at the wooden door waiting, seeing images of demons torturing souls in the grain of the wood.

After ten minutes with the doctor, I'm free to go into the community room. I grab another coffee. An orderly comes around on the hour to light cigarettes. People line up for their turn. I am one of them. At 8 a.m. breakfast comes. I'm always hungry, shoveling the food in as quickly as I can chew it. It's not bad for hospital food. Group therapy is at 10:30. My mother visits in the afternoons after work. She brings me cigarettes and books to read.

After 5 days I am cleared to go for walks outside. We're taken out as a group, the 5 of us who qualify, for a walk around the outside hospital grounds. There are trees and grass, and the air is fresh and heavy with the promise of rain. I am content to be where I am. I'm in no rush to leave, to go back to my life and all the questions that come with it.

Back in the room, my roommate is angry. She is yelling and slamming the door of her wardrobe repeatedly. I sit in my chair and try to read. I wonder what has set her off this time. Two nurses come in and take her away. I don't see her again.

In the community room I get a cigarette lit. There is a woman staring at me. She looks like an aged and shrunken version of my mother, just a bit in the face. Her eyes search mine. "Didn't I meet you back in Australia?" I flashback to my hallucination of the desert and my tank.

"What? No, I don't think so."

She smiles at me, her eyes look like they know something I don't. "My mistake." She walks away and I'm shaking.

The days go by, meds, doctor visits, cigarettes, meals, group therapy, all flowing together. I am compliant in all things. I do not make trouble. I am going through the motions amicably, waiting to be better. That's how this is supposed to work. I follow the rules, and they make me well.

He visits. He tells me that we will be married just as soon as I get out of here. They will never be able to take me away again. He seems angry that I've been kept in as long as I have. He has enough anger for both of us.

On the twelfth day they release me back into the wild. I've gained eight pounds. I have taken well to therapy and been cooperative. There is nothing more they can do for me inside. I will see my doctor once a month. I will take my meds.

Don't they know you're still mad?

Chapter 14

I go back to him. When I let him touch me, my skin crawls. I search back in my mind to try to figure out when lust became loathing. When did it all go wrong? I cannot find it. I cannot tell him. I do not want to hurt him. I do not love him.

He is true to his word and everything is already planned out. My mother takes me out to look for a wedding dress. She looks concerned. The weight of all the things she wants to say but won't hangs in the air between us.

She doesn't want you to go through with this.
Why are you going through with this?

It's a good question I have no answers for. I'm supposed to want this. I'm supposed to be in love, we've been engaged for a year and a half. This is what people do. Mostly it's just easier to go along. If I just keep doing what everyone tells me to, I don't have to think. Thinking is difficult, and scary. It's better just to let it all happen and worry about the basics.

We go to the mall. It's prom dress season, and the shops are full of formal looking dresses to choose from, although the selection in white is scant. I take a few into the dressing room while my mother waits dutifully outside. I pick the one on sale as it fits the best. I model it for her. Her smile doesn't reach her eyes. She pays for it and we drive off to the local florist.

Chapter 15

It is May, and I'm standing outside the Justice's office in my white JC Penny prom dress. Alexandra is smiling at me. My parents are standing around, chatting. My flowers match my bright pink shock of hair. He looks nervous. Maybe he's starting to catch on to what an absolute mistake this is. I can't be the only one. Everyone looks so somber in their formal wear, and there is me with bright pink hair and a wedding dress and combat boots.

It looks like this is it. I'm really doing it.

The doors open, and I fall.

Make a choice

S

For once in your life.

p

Let the chips fall where they may

l

Let the walls crumble at your feet

i

Cause as much chaos and destruction
As you need.

t

Better to watch the world burn
By your own hand

e

Than to stand by idly
While you drown in your own...

r

inertia

we

all

fall

down

Chapter 1

We don't really have a reception. Everyone comes to his house, our house, I guess it is now. We have a keg of beer, and some sandwiches, some chips. It's all very budget. The weather is nice enough, and we sit on a couch in the enclosed back porch, rolling a joint, drinking and smiling at all our well-wishers. There are a lot more people here than there were at the wedding.

I sit back and watch people drinking and eating and wonder what the point of it all is. There is little chance of this lasting. There isn't going to be a happily ever after. I get up and walk around, saying hello to people I haven't seen since high school. "Thanks for coming!" I smile. I probably seem almost normal. I make my way into the house and back to the bedroom. I close the door and lay on the bed and fall asleep.

I have always been a bit of a romantic- love, truth, and beauty. The importance of emotions above logic. That sort of thing. At least intellectually. But here I am, ignoring every gut instinct, clinging to a thing with no truth in it at all. I think maybe he is a bit of a romantic too. He seems to be convinced that this marriage will fix me. That his 'love' will be enough.

Summer goes by slowly. Everyday seems to be a test of my will to survive. I'm locked inside my head with this brain that simply will not function as it's meant to. I have never been more unhappy.

It's a bitter November evening when I go to CVS with my mother-in-law. She's shopping for something, I don't know what, I don't really pay much attention to what's going on around me these days. I just wander around in a sort of daze. I look through all the travel sized bits, and I'm holding a bottle of bath oil when she asks me if I need anything.

"No, I'm good."

"Okay, it's time to go, then." She finishes paying for whatever she's picked up, and I follow her out the door. An alarm starts blaring, and the security guy runs up and grabs me. The bath oil is still in my hand, I'm not trying to hide it, I've just forgotten I was holding it at all. Doris tries to explain to them that I'm ill, she'll pay for it, but they don't want to hear it. They're going to make an example out of me for trying to steal a three-dollar bottle of bath oil.

They bustle me to a room in the back where I am told I have to wait for the police. Doris looks horrified. I sit and wait, staring at a blank patch of the wall, my mind wandering to parts unknown.

The cops come and Doris tries once again to reason with them. The officer says there really isn't anything he can do, if CVS want to press charges for petty theft, he has to comply.

We drive down to the station and the police take my information. It's not a proper arrest, but I will have to pay a $200 fine to the courthouse after my case comes up. For now they release me into Doris' custody, and we go home.

My mother pays the fine. My husband berates me for putting his mother through that. I just sit silently as he yells. What can I say? I would feel terrible if my meds let me feel things, but I've been numb for months. He finally yells himself out, the futility of his anger robbing it of its heat.

It's Christmas time when he decides he's had enough. My marriage lasts all of six months before it falls apart. He tells me he thinks I should move back home to my parents' house, and the hot tears that slide down my face are born of humiliation, rather than heartbreak. I argue even though I knew this day would come. I go through all the motions of trying to cling on to something that no longer exists, and I don't think I even want. I look down at my holiday sweater and a sour taste assaults my mouth. The happiest time of the year.

The meds have quieted me down. I feel like I've got lead weights strapped to my arms and legs all the time. I drag myself around, still vaguely lost, but functioning. The voices are quiet, but my thoughts don't quite match up. I am perpetually confused and zoned out. Sometimes I smell things that aren't there, most often shit or fire. It usually passes quickly, but it's awful and scary when it happens.

None of my friends come around, and very few of his. I feel isolated and judged. Always judged. Some of it is just the delusions, but some of it is him. As if I've done this *to* him. How dare I lose my mind?

I pack up my comic books and clothes. There isn't much else I own, so it all fits in a couple of garbage bags. I drag them to his mother's car, and he drives me back to my parent's house, the little blue bungalow by the lake. He watches from behind the steering wheel as I struggle to empty the car of my belongings. I shut the door, and he drives off, leaving me there to pull out my keys and let myself inside.

My room is, as always, unchanged. I suspect my parents were waiting for this to happen. Why rearrange the room when I would need it again so soon?

I shove the bags of clothes in the closet and flop down on my bed. My mom and stepdad are both still at work, so the house is quiet. I light a cigarette and stare at the ceiling. I am feeling lost and sorry for myself. I've just been dumped by a guy I don't even like, let alone love, and somehow, it's destroying me. I need to find something to do with myself. I cannot just sit around the house, and I'm not really capable of holding down a job. My mother comes up with the answer. Cosmetology school.

It's perfect for me. I already cut and dye my own hair regularly. Why not learn how to do it properly? Go to school, get my license, and someday get a job. My mother promises me if I graduate, she will pay back my loan.

It's my chance for some sort of future, and I take it. I don't have any real aspirations, at this point. No dreams, and I haven't been able to envision a future for myself in - ever.

The local beauty school is in Grimsburg. My mom drops me off every morning with my kit and my manikin head and a packed lunch. The other girls there are intimidating, all long hair and manicured nails. They look like future hairstylists. I have a green mohawk and don't wear makeup. Under my apron I wear old man trousers and t-shirts two sizes too small.

I ignore the thought that everyone is judging me and throw myself into my studies. After a few weeks of theory, we move downstairs to the salon proper and start practicing on our manikins. Each week we learn a new haircut, and our manikin's hair gets slowly but surely shorter. We learn to do roller sets, then perms. Twice a week we do nails, and facials.

It doesn't take long before I make friends, Annie and Lisa. We set up our manikins together so we can gossip while we work. We go out on our lunch breaks together. They don't seem to think I'm overly weird. I guess maybe the meds are working.

Before long, we begin working on actual clients. It's mainly roller sets on older ladies, with the occasional trim. Every once in a while, someone comes in wanting a perm. I do a few of them during my time on the floor, and actually get asked to show another student how to do it when he gets a client. It makes me feel good, knowing I'm good at something.

I change my hair so often; I've taken to shaving it all off every few weeks. I go blonde, violet, apricot. We try to do leopard spots. Each time on a half inch of hair. It's more fun than doing it to the manikins.

Chapter 2

I see my psychiatrist once a month. The same one who diagnosed me in the hospital. He is kind, and encourages me to get out more, to meet people and do things. He can see my progress even when I cannot. I keep on taking my meds, I keep trying to be well. I'm not sure it's working, but I do keep trying.

School keeps my days busy, but I am isolated in the evenings. I don't know anyone my age locally, and I tend to keep to myself. The winter feels long and cold. I read a lot of books.

Spring rolls out slowly in Sayersville. The ice-covered dirt roads start to melt and become wheel rutted mud pits. The grass on the baseball field is slowly revealed again as the snow recedes, and the trees start to regain their leaves. The days grow longer, and I sneeze a lot.

May rolls around, and my husband decides we should go out to dinner for our anniversary. I think it's stupid, but he's paying, so I go and order myself a steak. He owes me a good meal anyway. He picks me up and drives me to a restaurant near my parents' house. He's in a good mood, laughing and smiling. Sometimes I think he is the crazy one. Who takes their estranged wife out for an anniversary dinner? I eat my dinner in silence while he tells me stories about his customers at Blockbuster. When I'm done, I ask him to take me home.

The weather heats up, eventually, and I decide to go to the beach at the lake. The beach has actual sand, just around this small section of the shore. I'm not sure where they got it from, but it's perfect for pretending you're near an ocean. The lake has no tide, but at least you can swim in it. Not that I ever do. It's murky and you can't see through the water, so I pass on that. I put down a towel and lay out in the sun.

There is a group of teenagers there, younger than me, but only by a few years. One of them comes over and introduces himself.

"Hi, I'm Lucas. I like your hair, it's cool. What's your name?" Lucas tells me he's 15 (he isn't) and that he goes to the same high school I went to. We chat about teachers and what classes he has. He introduces me to his brother and friends, and we all sit around, enjoying the summer sun and just being kids. When the sun finally sets, I tell Lucas where I live, and invite him to come stop by whenever he likes.

He shows up the following day, and the one after that, and before you know it, we're inseparable. Suddenly I am part of the large group of teenagers that roams the streets of Sayersville. It's a backwoods kind of town, in the middle of nowhere, and most of them are too young to drive, so we stick together. It's nice to feel so alone no longer.

They're a fun group of kids, and they accept me into their fold quickly. We hang out at the gas station parking lot, or down by the lake, some of the boys doing tricks on their skateboards, the rest of us just standing around, chatting and taking the piss out of each other. It's all fun and games until I see Dean. He's tall, with wavy blond hair and blue eyes. He is kind to me and doesn't seem to think I'm strange. When he looks at me, I melt.

Dean insists on walking me home that evening. I'm older than him and absolutely no one is around, but it's dark and he's feeling protective, so I let him. We talk and it's all very light and easy. I'm sad when he doesn't try to kiss me.

It's a week of him walking me home before I realize he's been getting in trouble to do it. He's been walking me home at ten, which is his curfew. He gets grounded for three days, and after that I insist on walking *him* home. We take the back way, down Golf Course Road past dilapidated old barns and wide fields. When we get to the highway he needs to cross to get to his backyard, he insists I stay. We kiss, finally, and he runs across the road, stopping to look back and wave from the far side. It is 9:55. I walk back home, giddy from that kiss like I haven't been in ages.

Lucas's brother begins showing up at my house. He likes to hang around and dig through my comic book collection. Sometimes he comes around when I'm out with Lucas and asks my mom if he can wait for me. She lets him, and I come home to find him sitting on my bed, playing video games.

"Who even let you in here?" I ask, annoyed that he's in my personal space.

"Your mom. Hey, do you want to hear the new CD I bought yesterday?"

"Not really! I kind of want to get changed and be alone."

Peacock laughs. He never seems to take the hint. I sigh and flop down on the far end of the bed. Lucas and I started calling him Peacock, I don't really remember why. It annoys him, which I guess is the point. He doesn't really get along with his brother. But he really likes my things and seems to think that we're friends. I light a cigarette and watch him play some video game I didn't even know I owned.

The Poconos are a really picturesque, postcard kind of place, but they are unbearably boring if you aren't the outdoorsy type. There are trees, and rolling hills, rivers and creeks, mountains, and trails, but not a whole hell of a lot else. When you're in Sayersville everything is a 15–20-minute drive away, and none of it is very interesting. If you're too young to drive, you're stuck with what's nearby. In my case, that was Sayers Lake, a gas station, a baseball field, a few bars, and not much else.

Having a friend group makes it all seem less like a punishment. I think back to my childhood, growing up in northern New Jersey, being able to ride my bike to the mall, or sneak on a train and wind up in NYC. There were parks and people and places to go. For some god-awful reason I had elected to give it all up and move here. And it *was* up to me, in the end. My mother had offered to stay in Jersey until I finished high school. I had had enough of the small-town mentality I had grown up in and for some inexplicable reason agreed to move to an even smaller town, miles from anywhere.

Chapter 3

Lucas's birthday rolls around, and I'm excited for his big sixteenth, until I talk to Peacock. Apparently, Lucas is turning fifteen, and has been lying to me about it for months. I'm hurt, but I get over it quickly. Would I have hung out with him if I'd known he was only fourteen when we met? I can't really say. But I'm glad I did. He's one of my best friends, and life would be a whole lot more boring without him.

I hang out with Dean a lot. We go to his house and watch skateboarding videos and kiss. He agrees to teach me to skate, and I manage to stand on his board and ride it without falling off. I think about him constantly, but I'm painfully aware he doesn't see me that way. He calls me up to tell me about a girl at school he has a crush on. My friend Tom's older sister. I thank him for the information and hang up.

The next time my husband calls, looking to see me, I go to him. I'm not sure if I'm doing it out of spite or some other reason, but I go in knowing full well I'll regret it. We watch some football game and drink beer and I feel like I've given up. This is all there is for me, this is all I deserve. Who needs happiness? What is love? I don't know, but they're things meant for other people. We have sex on the couch, and it feels obligatory. Just going through the expected motions.

Why am I even here?

Lucas and I are laying on a blanket at the baseball field watching fireworks When we meet a couple of twin brothers, Jason and Jared. Their grandmother owns a little summer bungalow just down the dirt road from my parents. They are up visiting from NJ. We wind up going back to their place, where they smoke us up and we watch TV together. We trade stories and just hang out. By morning it feels like we've known each other for years.

One night at Jason and Jared's place, I meet a boy named Kyle. He has blond hair and glasses and dresses in all black. We talk for hours, then make out on the couch. I give him my number, which turns out to be a huge mistake. He calls me incessantly and gets angry when he finds out I've spoken to my husband. I cut him off completely after a week. We never speak again, but his friend Lacy still hangs around. Lacy reminds me of myself, she is young and a little angry and not very happy with who she is. Everyone thinks she's cool, but I have this weird feeling about her.

I'm at beauty school and both of my friends have already finished their hours. I only have a week or so left myself, I can't really believe how quickly it's all gone. I go outside to eat my lunch alone thinking maybe I'll walk over to the benches near the courthouse. There, parked outside the building, is my husband. I walk over to the car and tap on his window.

"What are you doing here?"

"I want to talk," he gestures to the passenger seat, "get in."

I sigh and get in the car. I don't really want to talk to him. I don't even want to see him. It's always messy, and painful and he always wants something from me. I have already given him everything. I'm empty now. I just want to eat my lunch in peace and live my life.

"So, I spoke to a lawyer," he says, bursting out in tears.

My face falls. I can't deal with this. I know he feels guilty, like he should have been able to fix me, or some dumb shit like that. "You talked to a lawyer and now you're sad. Why are you crying?"

His hands are gripping the steering wheel and his knuckles are white. He's shaking his head. He doesn't seem to be able to speak.

"What, you still love me? Is that it?"

He's looking at me, willing me to do all the talking. I don't want to say it, but the words tumble out.

"You want to try again." It's not a question, but he nods at me like I need an answer.

I shrug. "Okay."

Chapter 4

By the weekend I am moved back in. It's all surreal, like returning to the scene of an accident where you almost died. The shapes and colors all jump out at you like you're seeing them in a funhouse mirror. I feel vaguely ill at all times, like I shouldn't be here. I'm not sure what it is in me that insists on seeing this through.

My first realization is that alcohol has become a daily thing here. He's buying a thirty pack of cheap beer every couple of days. I'm not one to point fingers, but it seems excessive. His best friend Todd comes over daily. We drink and play cards and wrestling or football blares from the TV. I can't say I enjoy any of it, but it passes the time.

He tells me it's okay to invite my friends around, he knows I must miss them. And I do. I call Lucas and we drive down to Sayersville to pick him up for the night. We all get a bit drunk, and Lucas runs down the street cuddling a couch cushion and calling it his lovey. I missed him but I feel terrible at how drunk he's gotten. I love my friends, but I want to protect them from this place. It ruined me, and I fear it will do the same to them, somehow. I start hanging out with them back in Sayersville instead of bringing them here.

The resort he works at is hiring housekeepers, so I go apply for a job. Alex works there as well, but on the phone lines as a telemarketer. I'm not actually sure what it is she sells, maybe vacation properties, but she's really good at her job and makes decent money. She's always on the leaderboard, top seller of the week. She has a really good phone voice; I've heard it a thousand times.

I get the job cleaning rooms and we discuss saving up for a move. We could easily afford to get a car and an apartment in Grimsburg, but it's the mid-nineties and my husband wants to move to Seattle. I agree, doubting we'll ever manage to save up enough. The truth is, I have no intention of going anywhere with him, let alone to the other side of the country. It all just feels like make believe.

The job lasts a little while, maybe a month. I clean rooms quietly, it doesn't matter that I'm a bit lost, I just go through the motions. I don't have to talk to anyone, so it works for me. Then the incident happens.

We had been drinking, of course. He said something, and I laughed at him. It wasn't funny, whatever he'd said. It wasn't a joke, and I was laughing at him, not with him. It was a nasty laugh. I'd found my bitterness escaping more and more and this was definitely one of those times.

He jumped on me, rolling me over and pinning me to the couch on my back. Then he punched me in the face, over and over. Not too hard. It didn't hurt really, not at first. But he just kept going. Todd was there, and he just sort of stared in disbelief, I guess. Finally he jumped up and left the room. Todd followed him out. I didn't know what to think, but unfortunately for him, it left bruises.

He took me to work the next day. I don't know why. Maybe he didn't notice. He certainly wasn't looking for me in the face. Alex was the first to notice.

"What the fuck happened?"

I told her. Word got around, and by the end of the day, he was fired. Alex drove me to her house, where she took about fifteen pictures of my face from different angles. Afterwards, I made her drive me back to his house. She didn't want to, but I convinced her it would be okay, nothing else was going to happen. I called up and quit the next day. I couldn't face going back there. The stares, the questions.

Our fights get uglier. One day we are sitting in the yard with friends, drinking as usual. He calls me a slut and worse as I'm walking away. I sit down on the grass and start taking off my combat boot. He is still laughing when I walk up behind him and swing my boot like a baseball bat, connecting with his back. He yells out in anger.

"Fuck you!" I yell back.

Our friends are the only thing stopping him from retaliation. One of them physically holds him back and talks us both down off the proverbial ledge. I'm probably lucky not to get the shit beaten out of me.

These flare ups happen from time to time. No one is happy and I guess we see each other as the root of our unhappiness. I don't know why I stay and keep trying to make things work. I just can't seem to bring myself to give up on whatever it is I think we once had.

In October, my mother calls. She needs to come get me, it's my cat, Rascal. He's had another seizure, but this time his back legs have stopped working. He is an old cat, we rescued him as a kitten just before I turned two. I decide it's time.

We take him to the vet, and I hold him, petting him and looking in his eyes as the drugs hit him. Then he is gone. I wrap him in my flannel, and we drive back to my husband's house. He hands me a shovel and a bottle of wine, and I go out into the backyard and dig at the cold, hard ground. I cry the entire time, swigging from the wine bottle and chopping at the dirt.

We take turns, and it takes hours, but we finally bury Rascal in the backyard, not far from his old cat Buffy. My hands are caked in dirt and my face is red when I tumble into bed that night.

I go to my cosmetology school graduation ceremony. Because the school is hours based, (you need 1,250 hours in a licensed school in the state of Pennsylvania), everyone finishes at different times, and they hold one graduation ceremony per year. So basically, I've been done for months by the time I graduate. It's nice to see everyone that I've fallen out of touch with. My mother and Lucas come to cheer me on. My husband has work, but I don't really want him there anyway. This is a separate part of my life, and I'm happy to keep him out of it.

One day I am hanging out at Jason and Jared's house. He comes to pick me up. Lacy is there, and she gets to talking with him. When he drives us back home, she comes along. They get along really well. Too well. He's twenty-two, and I'm not sure how old she is. Fourteen, fifteen? He looks at her like a shark. My stomach turns.

She hangs around for weeks. She tells her mom we're younger than we are, but to be honest, her mother doesn't seem that concerned. We drive off with her daughter and she stays at our house for days at a time. I know things are heading in a terrible direction. Lacy barely ever spoke to me before this, and now suddenly she's acting like my best friend. It gets to the point where my stomach drops every time I enter a room, unsure of what I'm going to find.

I wake up one morning on the couch, after a night of drinking and wander over to the bedroom for a change of clothes. That's when it finally happens. They're in our bed and he is completely naked. She is wearing a long t-shirt. I walk over to his sleeping form and punch him right in the face. Then I walk out into the kitchen and call my mother.

I pack up some clothes in a bag and sit on the couch and wait. He comes out of the bedroom. We scream at each other. Lacy looks scared. My mother pulls up twenty minutes later, and I climb into her car with a garbage bag full of clothes. We drive off, and I can't see through the tears. Our second try lasts all of a few months.

I can't understand why he does these things to me. Why does he show up in tears just to use me as some kind of bait for young girls? All this time, I thought it was my sickness telling me that he didn't care, but apparently it really *was* my intuition. I find it so hard to know what is real and what is not at this point. Which feelings do I believe?

More to the point, why do I allow him to use me like this? Why do I think things will ever change? He is a terrible, selfish person, and maybe I am too, but I'm playing little league and he's a goddamn pro. Why did I even agree to this in the first place? I do not like him. I had a perfectly reasonable life going on without him. School, friends, it was all going fine. Why is there something in me so desperate for male approval that I would walk away from all that for this absolute garbage example of humanity? I'm not sure I'll ever figure it out.

Chapter 5

They wind up dating for at least six months. Our mutual friends insist on telling me every gory detail. I don't know who I hate more, him or me. Probably him, but only just. I feel responsible for exposing this poor girl to him. I know she must think she knows what she's doing but in my mind, he is simply a monster now.

I get a job apprenticing at a salon while I wait to test for my license. The first few days I just sweep up hair and answer phones. On the third day, a man comes in for a haircut, and I give it to him, although the head stylist checks my work before he leaves. I am a bundle of nerves the entire time, but it seems to go off okay.

On day five of my new job, my mom and Lucas come to pick me up from work. They park outside and keep flipping me off and giggling every time I look over at them. We are closed, and I am giving the floor one final sweep when I flip them the bird in return. Unfortunately, the owner sees me. After a ten-minute tirade, I am sent out the door, jobless. I decide doing hair is probably not for me.

For a while, I flit around aimless and angry. I date a guy called Greg for a few weeks. We meet at the lake, and he asks me out. One night he picks me up and takes me to a party at his apartment. He disappears for a while and leaves me surrounded by complete strangers. When he finally comes back, he's wearing a wig and a dress. He walks up to me and says, "What's your name, I'm a man...duh."

I find him off-putting and obnoxious. He drives me home and tries to kiss me in his car, parked by the lake. I turn my head away and tell him I think we should just be friends. He asks me why he's always attracted to skinny little girls who look like boys. He shouts it at me, spittle flying everywhere. I grab his wig and run from the car, run all the way home.

I can't figure out why I do this to myself. I continually find myself with men I don't even like. The only prerequisite seems to be that they are interested in me. I suppose I don't think I'm worth much. I certainly don't treat myself like I do.

The wig becomes a mainstay of my wardrobe. I give it a little trim, and it looks like Uma Thurman's hair in Pulp Fiction. I name her Mandy and I wear her whenever I feel like changing up my look.

One weekend my parents go away, and Lucas stays over to keep me company. We order pizza and watch movies, waiting for the sun to set. When nightfall comes, we head out to the Lake with some screwdrivers and set about trying to remove some parking signs from the fence around the lake. We've almost got one loose when Lucas stops and starts shouting at me.

"Fru, we have to go back! I'm lactose intolerant! Fru, run!!"

Before I can ask him what the hell he's talking about, he's running back to my house, so I run after him. We get back and he spends the next half an hour in the toilet. The signs are left hanging on the fence, and I sit up against the bathroom door laughing until I cry.

Lucas never fails to surprise me. One day I come home to find my room tidied and my bed made. In the middle of my carefully arranged pillows is a teddy bear, with an open notebook propped up against it. The page reads: I am gay, please love me.

"Mom," I call out, "Did anyone come over while I was out?"

"Yeah, Lucas came around saying he'd left his hat in your room. He stayed in there for about fifteen minutes and then left. Why, what's up?"

"He's finally come out! I'm so proud of him!"

Chapter 6

Somedays I just walk around by myself, trying to clear my head. My thoughts are still jumbled and disconnected. I function okay in the world, but I have a hard time on my own. The quiet just leaves me to fixate on my broken brain and splintered thoughts.

Dean and I are constantly on and off, but we're never really on. We just sort of hook up occasionally. I try not to want more, but I do. Eventually I start avoiding him. It's just easier.

I am, once again, lost and directionless. When my mother suggests I take a night class at the local community college, just to give myself something to do, I think I might as well. I sign up for a creative writing class. That's where I meet Sal.

Sal is in his early 30's, over a decade older than me. We're both just looking for something to do, I guess. The class starts off with a round of introductions, the teacher directing us all to share a little bit about ourselves. When my turn comes, I sit back in my chair and say, "I am a schizophrenic, and my husband is screwing a teenager, and my mother thinks night classes will somehow solve all my problems, so here I am."

Sal laughs while all the later-in-life housewives look scandalized, staring at me with wide eyes and open mouths. That pretty much seals it. We exchange numbers at the end of class.

Maybe Sal is interested in me at first, but I don't notice. Or maybe I just ignore it. I'm so far from that mindset at this point, I really can't tell. What I need is a friend. Unlike a guy my age, he realizes this and doesn't make a move and make things awkward. We just hang out, talk about music and books, and get drunk. I sleep on his couch for the very first time ever, after an evening spent drinking screwdrivers and laughing.

Sal lives above a laundromat just off of Main Street. He works nights stocking at a supermarket, and I spend more and more of my time at his place. We listen to punk rock and drink vodka. He goes off to work, and I sit around his living room playing video games or reading Kerouac into the wee hours.

Soon a new coffee shop opens up in town. It's called Beans and it's only a ten-minute walk from Sal's house. Before long, everyone under the age of forty has discovered it. It becomes the place to hang out and meet up. They have live music on the weekends, and a poetry night in the back room on Thursdays. The shop is owned by a really lovely young gay couple, and it becomes the place to be.

I rarely get to see most of the Sayersville gang, except Lucas. I make new friends my own age and sort of settle into a new rhythm.

Poetry night gets popular, and a reporter from the Pocono Record comes down and does a whole article about Beans for the Local Living section. There is a huge picture of me, reading one of my poems, above the article. Alex cuts it out and calls to congratulate me.

The sandwich shop next door to Sal's house is hiring, and I decide to apply. I sleep on his couch more often than I sleep at home anyway. If I get a job, I can help pay for stuff and stop being such a sponge. Sal agrees it's a great idea.

Tip tap, yip yap
Caught inside
A mind trap.
Colors flash,
Meld and blend
Closing me
Inside again

a n d t h e n

What I feel and
What I see
Only ever known
to me.
You can try to
Understand
But we all die
alone, my friend.

Tip tap, yip yap
Caught inside
A mind trap.
Colors flash,
Meld and blend
Closing me
Inside again
What I feel and
What I see
Only ever known
to me.
You can try to
Understand
But we all die
alone, my friend.

Tip tap, yip yap
Caught inside
A mind trap.
Colors flash,
Meld and blend
Closing me
Inside again
What I feel and
What I see
Only ever known
to me.
You can try to
Understand
But we all die
alone, my friend.
splinter...

Chapter 1

My head feels like a kettlebell, my neck like it is about to snap from the weight of it. I'd been leaning over, head out the window screaming obscenities at Lacy, who my husband has been fucking for the past few months, as if it is this girl's fault. She's only fourteen, after all, maybe fifteen now. I'm crumpled on the floor, crawling across the room to the couch after a karmic gut punch. Sal is up like a flash and at my side.

"Are you okay?"

"I think I sprained my neck or something. Just give me a minute."

I sit, eyes swimming, trying to catch my composure.

"I need to lay down. Can you call next door and tell them I can't come in? I don't think I can stand up."

My third shift of training at the sandwich shop next door starts in under an hour and I can't even sit upright, let alone stand around making sandwiches. My first job in about a year. Sal walks over to the kitchen, and I sink down onto the sofa, head pounding in time with my heartbeat.

"They said if you don't come in today, you haven't got a job."

I grunt.

"Do you want me to call a doctor? I think I should call a doctor." Sal steps nervously back and forth between the couch and the phone.

"It's probably just a migraine. I need to sleep." I've had migraines for as long as I can remember, but never one like this. All I want to do is sleep, let my body do whatever it needs to. I pass out.

I wake to a gentle shake from Sal. "I'm going to work. Are you sure you don't want me to call you a doctor? Or your mom?"

"Nah, go on, I'll be okay." I hear his footsteps as he slowly crosses the room, and the click of the door.

I try to walk to the bathroom. *That's a negatory on the standing, Mags*. I retch into the toilet a few times then pull myself up to splash my face with cold water. I sit back hard on the tiles. *I think I might be dying.* The thought hangs there. I imagine Sal coming home to find me dead on his bathroom floor. A life cut short, dead too soon to join the 27 club. *Can't have that!* I drag myself back to the couch.

When I wake again, it's light out. I have no idea what time it is. Is Sal back? If so, he's sleeping. I stumble as quietly as possible to the phone and call my mother.

"Something is wrong, I need you to get me to the doctor."

"Well, that's not going to happen. It's Sunday. They're closed."

I sigh. “The emergency room then. Something is wrong.”

“Okay, I’ll come pick you up.”

The emergency room is packed, and every sound is absolute agony. Crumpling crisp packet, murmuring voices, the sharp pop of a soda can being opened. I’m writhing in the hard plastic chairs of the waiting room for hours, all the while wondering if I am really dying. My head thrums rhythmically.

When I’m finally seen, they have no clue what is wrong.

“I think I sprained my neck; my head feels like it weighs 40 lbs. and it’s pounding. I threw up.”

People come and go from my room. No one seems overly concerned. Eventually they decide to send me for a scan.

Suddenly I’m surrounded by concerned faces.

“It looks like a brain hemorrhage,” the doctor announces, “We’ll have to move her.”

Chapter 2

The local hospital is ill equipped to deal with a neurological problem of this severity, so a 30-minute ambulance ride it is.

Why does my brain hate me so much? First schizophrenia, now this.

I stare up at the ceiling and watch as the tubes and bags jostle about as we drive up the entrance ramp for the highway.

The meds had eventually worked as well as they were going to. It took two years, but the voices had quieted, and the delusions had mostly gone. People no longer believed me when I introduced myself as clinically insane. They would laugh it off and say that we're all a little crazy. I was passing out there in the real world.

What a perfect time to die.

I am wheeled into a private room directly across from the nurse's station. The room is spacious, with a sink and cabinets and a TV hanging from the ceiling. A nurse sets up my IV, shows me the call button and doses me with morphine. I feel the warmth crawl up my arm and settle over my body. I sleep, my dreams hazy and indistinct, one bleeding into the next.

The neurologist is there when I wake. He is an attractive man with a smooth face, silver hair, and kind eyes. "Well, Maggie, the good news is, if you were going to die, you'd have done so before you made it here. The bleed has stopped, but we have to keep an eye on how your brain is reabsorbing the blood. It's a very tricky time, so you're going to have to stay in bed until we're sure things are taking care of themselves."

The relief hits me like a wave. "I can do that."

"That's the spirit. We'll send you down for another scan tomorrow to see how things are progressing. You just relax and let your body heal."

The next few days pass in a haze of painkiller fueled dreams. I sleep mostly, only waking up to find Sal, or my mom, or food waiting for me. Only once did I wake to find my husband before me.

"What do you want?"

"You could have died." He is crying.

"I didn't." I look out the window, longing for a smoke. What right does he have to even be here? "What do you care, anyway?"

"I still love you.

"Go tell your girlfriend." I close my eyes hoping he'll be gone when I open them again. I have enough problems. I do not want him, but I cannot bring myself to let go. His presence is an unwelcome reminder that I am still all wrapped up in him.

More often I wake to find Lucas by my bedside. He skips school three days running to come visit me. The drugs keep me from staying awake long, but he's there often enough that I'm surprised when he's not.

I wake to a nurse topping up my morphine. I flip through the channels and catch The Empire Strikes Back right at the beginning. I snuggle into my pillows and drift off as Luke gets lost on Hoth.

A voice asks me if I want more painkillers.

"Yes please."

I feel the familiar warmth from my iv, then suddenly my stomach flips. Everything feels wrong. My eyes snap open. I look to the television. Empire is *still* on. Luke still has both hands. It's too soon. I grab an empty bowl and begin to throw up.

I throw up 6 times in the next hour. My nurse is getting tired of me ringing for help, but I'm not allowed out of bed to sick up in a toilet like a normal person. I need to keep using this tiny bowl and he needs to keep cleaning it out. It's a hellish hour for us both, but we survive. Years later I will be told my records say I'm allergic to morphine, even though I was fine on it for days until they double dosed me.

Eventually, they let me leave.

Chapter 3

I walk to the neurology center with my mother. I spent six days in a drug induced haze before they finally allowed me to leave the hospital.

"Let's go see Dr. Hottie" my mother giggled.

The doctor awaits us with a warm smile. "How are we feeling, Maggie?"

"Not bad, Dr. Casavetes. Happy to be out of bed."

The MRI scans are all hung up on a lighted board for us to view. We sit and stare as the doctor picks up his pen.

"This is your bleed, when you first came in." He says, pointing to one of the pictures. "You had an AVM, probably from birth. A knot of blood vessels right here." He points to a spot almost directly in the middle of my brain. "Lucky for you they were only blood vessels. Pressure built up and caused a rupture. Now, as you can see, this is fairly central in your brain. I'm recommending radiosurgery to turn this AVM into, well, basically scar tissue. It's an outpatient procedure which takes a few hours."

Radio surgery will involve a big metal halo screwed into my skull. It'll be held in place by the machine that will zap my brain *just so* to turn a very small area into scar tissue. It sounds gnarly and scary but loads better than dying.

“I want you to take a month off of work. Take it easy. Spend a lot of time in bed. Your brain is still healing.”

“I don’t think that’ll be a problem.” I laugh. I don’t even know if I have a job, at this point.

The ride back home is quiet. I stare out the window, watching the trees pass by, wondering if my luck is good or bad. I’m alive, that definitely goes in the “good” column. My brain seems to want to kill me though, one way or another. That’s a tick in the “bad” column. The car pulls up to the little blue bungalow near the lake, my parent’s house.

My room seems untouched. Everything is right where I left it. Posters still cover the walls, my CDs stacked next to the CD player, even my closet is still a mess.

My mother stands in the doorway.

“Mags, when was the last time you took your pill?”

I think about it for a few seconds, “Saturday. Last Saturday.”

My mother smiles, “You seem good. How do you feel?”

“Fine. Tired though, think I’ll take a nap. Dr.’s orders, you know.”

I wouldn’t take antipsychotic medication again for years to come. Eighteen of them, in fact.

I wake from a dream of a hotel room with a start. Except I can't move, and the dream is still happening, so maybe not really 'wake'. There are flowers in a pot on the wall. They are me, somehow, and I am them. They wither and rot and then come back to life and do it again. It feels ominous and full of secret meaning. When I can finally move again, I roll over and cry.

Why am I like this? Why can't anything be easy? My mind doesn't answer, so I get up, get changed and go to the kitchen for a drink. It's night now, the house is quiet. I grab a cake and some iced tea and head back to my room.

It's so quiet. The voices aren't answering and as much as I hate to admit it, it feels lonely. Maybe sanity will be boring compared to what I've become used to. I twitch. *No! This is good!*

I look at the pill bottle on my dresser. *I don't need you.* That feels good. I walk over to my comic book box and dig out my Johnny the Homicidal Maniac graphic novel and settle down in bed to relax.

When I rest, the sleep paralysis returns. It's been this way for days. This time it's a siren wailing.

Wheeee-oooo-wheeee-oooo-wheee-oooo!

The end of the world. Faces of people I love float around me. *Why did you do this?* Their eyes accusing. My heart pounds, but I'm oddly calm. It's happening so often that I'm growing used to it. My shadow friend cavorts around the walls of my room winking at me. It's over.

Chapter 4

Two weeks later, the sleep paralysis has died down and I'm ready for a night out. Poetry night at the Beans, my favorite night of the week. I haven't been there for over a month now. I don't tell anyone I'm coming back. I just want to show up and read my newest poem, not answer loads of awkward brain questions.

I pull out a razor and touch up around my mohawk. My hair needs a new dye job, but it's going to have to wait until I start working again. A mint chocolate hot chocolate from Beans is about as far as my funds will stretch. I throw on my favorite plaid trousers and a Goodwill tee shirt, stick up my mohawk with shaving cream and gel, and head out the door.

I get to Beans a little early so I can get my drink and find a good seat in the back room. That's where poetry night happens. In a small, deep room with couches and chairs and a low table. There are paintings on the wall and a heavy drape cordoning it off from the coffee shop proper. It is really *really* nice to be back.

A few people are already there. Tom is playing acoustic guitar and singing a Hole song. I join in, "Rose white, rose red. Rose up in my head. Rose white, rose red."

"Maggie!" Tom stops playing. "How are you? What happened with your..." he gestures with the guitar at his head.

"My brain went a little explodey, yeah." I set my cup down carefully before plopping on the couch. "I'm okay now though."

"Everybody was saying you were going to die and stuff; it was crazy."

"Still here amongst the living." I sip my hot chocolate. "Only me, right?"

People begin to trickle in. Tom goes back to playing his guitar and I settle back into the couch, flipping through my notebook. It feels good to be back here, doing normal things.

"Hey Maggie, there's a band playing Beans this Saturday, you coming?"

"I am now!"

Saturday night is a different scene. The seats outside are filled, as is the coffee house proper. The doors are open, and the music spills out into the street. Sal waves me over when I arrive.

"There's this lady in the band who says she's psychic. She read my palm for a cigarette; you should talk to her!"

I laugh but am intrigued. "Okay, you introduce me, and I'll get her to read my palm."

I push my way inside and up to the counter to order the usual. The band has a sort of rollicking jam band sound. Not really my thing, but good for a night out. I grab my order and head back out to Sal's table.

"How're you feeling?" he asks, looking for signs of weakness. He seems to feel guilty.

"I'm fine. Really. I promise."

"Just don't overdo it. Are you even supposed to be out?"

"How is sitting at a coffee shop more taxing than sitting on my mom's couch? It's fine. I'm not dying anytime soon. Besides, my neurologist said to have caffeine at the first sign of a headache. If anything, this is *good* for me."

The band takes a break and wanders outside to mix with the crowd. Sal jumps up and walks over to a lady with long gray matted locks and a long, drapey dress. "This is the friend I was telling you about, Maggie. She'd love a reading if you're up for it."

"Hi Maggie, I'm Elise. Can I see your hands?" I proffer my hands and await my fortune. "I see witches run in your family. It's in the knuckles." I think about my grandmother, who always has this sixth sense whenever anything out of the ordinary is going on. She'll call out of nowhere the second anything occurs.

"Maggie, you're not crazy." She looks at me pointedly. "There is something about you, it's making these strange things happen all around you and to you. But it is already resolving itself. You're not crazy, even though you think you are." Elise takes a cigarette from Sal and turns to walk away. "Nice meeting you, Maggie." She walks off.

"What did you tell her about me?" I turn to Sal. "Tha had to be some kind of set up."

"Nothing, I swear! I just told her I had a friend that could use a psychic." Sal puts his hands up.

"I don't believe you." I'm shaking. "What the fuck."

Chapter 5

I'm watching TV at my mom's house when the phone starts to ring. I stare at it, willing it to stop, but it doesn't, so I answer.

"Hello?"

"We need to talk." It's my husband. Soon to be ex-husband.

"We really, really don't."

"If you don't want to try again, why not file for divorce?"

"Well let's see, my brain just exploded and I'm not back to work yet so I don't have $300. Does that answer your question, or do you want me to draw up a graph?"

"Come on Maggie. This is the first time you've seemed sane since we got married. Isn't it worth giving it another try? Let me come over, we can talk."

"We're talking now. If you're in a hurry to make it legal, do it yourself. Otherwise you can wait until I've gotten a few paychecks. Your choice."

I put down the phone. 'Let me come over' is just code for 'let's fuck', and I'd rather gouge my own eyes out than be with him. The last time I let him touch me, I counted every second, staring at the ceiling, willing it to be over. It felt like stepping in a puddle with socks on. Uncomfortable and weird. We split up twice already and tried again once as well. It didn't get any better. I can't forgive him for the way he watched me deteriorate and just sat by. The way he'd choked me on the floor. It all comes flooding back. I don't *want* to forgive him. I just want him out of my life. I hate that he's so smug. That he thinks I still want him. He was never who I thought he was. I loved a ghost. I can see that now, but he thinks he has me dickmatized or something. All he has over me is the time I wasted on him.

There's a knock at the door, it's Lucas.

"Hi, Fru," he says, calling me by the nickname only he uses,

"What's going on?"

We're joking and laughing and chatting. Lucas says he wants to try on one of my dresses.

"You're too big, Bazoozoo, you'll stretch it all to hell. Go try on one of mommy's."

Lucas runs to my mother's closet and begins searching for a dress. It takes a while because she's not really a dress person, but finally he finds one and puts it on. He's strutting around the living room, posing for me when my mother walks in the front door.

“LUCAS!” She shouts, in either shock or anger, possibly both. He runs for the bathroom and locks himself in as my mother chases him and begins banging on the door. “You come out here and take that dress off right now! I’m getting the frying pan!”

“I AM,” he yells through the door. I’m curled up on the couch laughing so hard I’m crying.

Contrary to her threats, when Lucas comes out of the bathroom, holding the balled-up dress in front of him like a flag of surrender, it’s a plastic spatula she smacks him with. Lucas heads for the front door, and out it so quickly, I don’t get to say goodbye.

Time for work. My mother had gone down to the sandwich shop while I was in the hospital and explained what had happened. The owners said I could come back to work when I was well again. Now I am set for my first non-training shift, complete with a lunch rush. My stomach tingles with nervous energy and I twitch a few times, but otherwise I’m ready to go.

The shift goes by in a flurry of rolls and meats and toppings. I make more sandwiches than I can count, but it all goes well. No messed-up orders, no complaints. No time to think about anything else. At the end of my shift the owner calls me over to ask about my head. I explain what an AVM is, and how I was born with it and it randomly burst. I tell her about the radio surgery in February, and how it’s a one-day procedure and I won’t have to miss any more work.

My twenty-first birthday is coming up. I've put aside an entire paycheck. The neurologist said to take it easy, but not *too* easy. Dr Casavetes is an absolute angel. Sal is working, but I've got a few other friends who are old enough to hit the bars with me. It's going to be a night to remember.

On the day, I get up and get dressed. I eat some cereal and dance around. The house is empty, so I blast 'Live Through This' by Hole in its entirety and throw myself into it with real abandon. When eleven am rolls around, I walk myself to the bar down the road and buy my first six pack. Blue Moon Belgian White. Then I walk back home happily with my legally procured alcohol.

I stick the beer in the fridge, leaving one out to drink. I sit on my bed and drink my beer and think about life. Twenty-one and I've already had a breakdown, a failed marriage, and a near death experience. *Well, got all that out of the way. I'm ready to have some fun now,* I think. A few nice easy years of working and hanging out with friends and just enjoying life sounds perfect.

The night turns out to be one of mildly drunken revelry. I drink cheap beer, play pool (badly) and laugh a lot. The problems of the last two years seem a million miles away. I sleep on Sal's couch for the first time since my brain hemorrhage. His present to me was a key to the apartment, so now I can crash any time I need to.

The weeks go by quickly. Work, Beans, Sal's couch, home when I have a few days off. I drink more hot chocolate than beer.

I begin to wonder where it's all heading.

Chapter 6

Cleveland.

Sal has three days off work, so we decide on taking a road trip. The destination needs to be within a day's drive, and neither of us have been to Cleveland before. We pack up our overnight bags and set off in Sal's black top, white '64 Mustang. We fill the long ride with chatter, chain smoke and a blaring radio. We laugh and sing.

Neither of us know where anything is in Cleveland. We drive around aimlessly looking for something interesting to do. Sal pulls up near a shop called Big Fun. It is filled with toys from our childhoods. I spy a wall full of metal lunchboxes and it fills me with joy. I'd owned at least four of these. They have every action figure I can remember, and a few that are before my time. The aisles are a jumble of old toys and gag gifts stacked so high I can't reach the top shelf. Sal buys some playing cards.

Next stop is the Museum of Art. We wander past paintings and statues while a security guard follows us everywhere. After a while, we tire of pretending to touch things, and head out to find a burger joint and eat something. That's when we realize we'd entered through an exit and never checked our bags. Innocent mistake.

We drive back early the next day, Bob Dylan serenading us on the ride. I stare out the window at plains and soft hills and farmland. Life was starting to get boring. Stuff needed to start happening quickly. Something in the peaceful morning air irritates me. It is too quiet, too green.

A ska band is playing a show down on Main Street. I decide to throw back a few beers and check them out. The crowd is filled with strangers. I dance until I'm flinging sweat around me in big fat droplets as I spin. The band is okay, nothing great but I don't care at this point. The trumpet player hits on me. I kiss him deeply. He's a sloppy kisser. When he asks for my number, I give it to him.

Ska boy calls me up the next day. He invites me up to his house, over an hour away. I get Sal to drop me off at a mall near his house. I don't know why I'm doing this. I do not like this boy at all, but he promised his brother would drive me home. It's not until Sal has left that I find out he means tomorrow. Another terrible decision for the books. I run out of a store while he's browsing and head to the pay phones.

I call my mother collect and beg her to come get me. I hide in the toilets for over an hour, waiting. Once again, I have gotten myself into a terrible situation someone else has to bail me out of. I am grateful for my support system.

Chapter 7

One night at Beans a woman comes up and asks what size I wear. Turns out she makes clothes, and thinks I'd make a good fitting model for an extra small. She can't pay me, but I can keep the clothes. I say "Yes" because saying "yes" to everything is the only way interesting things will ever happen.

Jessie works out of the basement of her house, not far from town. It's up on a hill, all stonework, and manicured gardens. I stand outside and ring the bell with sweaty hands. Jessie leads me downstairs to a stack of outfits laid out neatly on a table.

"Let me just get your measurements to start off with", Jessie grabs her measuring tape and gets straight to business. I try not to fidget while she whips the measuring tape out and around.

"You're pretty much exactly a

Juniors extra small. Here, try this on for me." She hands me a two-piece outfit, a black skirt and a purple top. I step behind a curtain and change clothes.

"You didn't wear a bra." Jessie frowned.

"I don't own one." I shrug.

Jessie checks the waist on the skirt and writes down some numbers in her notebook.

"Perfect fit. You can keep this one. Try on the pink dress next."

I leave a little over an hour later with 2 new outfits and a new adventure down in the books. My mother pulls up to give me a ride.

"How did it go?" she asks, pulling out of the driveway.

"Yeah, easy stuff. Just put on the clothes and stood around a lot."

"And how are we feeling about tomorrow?" Tomorrow is my radiosurgery. I am not looking forward to having a metal halo pinned to my skull.

"Yeah, fine." I look out the window.

Chapter 8

We arrive at the hospital at 9 and check in. I sit in the waiting room trying not to think too much about what is going to happen. After flipping through three magazines, someone finally comes to get me.

I change into a hospital gown. The nurse fiddles around giving me an IV. I hate needles. I've always always hated needles. Once when I was twelve I ran from a booster shot. I screamed when the nurse caught me. The pediatrician said I was old enough to go to a regular doctor after that. They didn't want me scaring the little kids.

I sit in a wheelchair, and they wheel me out to meet the radiosurgeon. He has warm brown hair, a full beard and twinkling blue eyes.

"Hi, I'm Dr. Coplan. I'll be in charge of your radiosurgery today." He sticks out a hand and I shake it. "We're going to have to shave a bit of your hair off here, doesn't look like that'll be much of a problem for you, though. Your mohawk is going to make my job easier." He smiles.

Dr. Coplan waits for the nurse to get done shaving the patches he needs, then pulls out a marker.

"I'm just going to mark your head up a bit. This won't hurt at all. While I'm doing that, our anesthesiologist will give you some meds, then inject your skull with anesthesia. The first one will pinch a bit, but you shouldn't feel much after that."

The painkillers hit quickly. True to the doctor's word, the first shot stings a bit, but by the time they move on to the next one, I can't feel a thing. I giggle and try to hold my head still. Soon they're fitting the halo around my head. It crosses just under my eyeline, cutting off my vision. There is a dull pressure as they pin it in place, and the halo itself feels heavy.

"You doing okay, Maggie?" Dr. Coplan asks.

I give him two thumbs up and giggle.

"Great. The nurse is just going to wheel you over to wait while we set everything up. We'll be with you soon."

They wheel me back to the room where my mother is waiting.

"Looks like you get to order lunch, Mags. hot dog, burger, or soup?"

I laugh. "Hot dog, definitely. It's the only one I have a chance at getting in my mouth like this. I giggle some more.

"Soup, for fuck's sake. How am I supposed to eat soup?"

"I would help you!"

A nurse walks in. "They're almost ready for you. We're going to wheel you out near the nurses."

There's a television at the nurse's station. It's playing some daytime talk show. The music catches me, and I start bobbing my head around thinking how good the drugs they have me on are.

The procedure goes well. I don't remember much. Some noise. Attempting to eat a hot dog. The weight of the halo disappearing and my head being wrapped in bandages. Then we're in the car and on the road going home. I'd scheduled four days off work just in case anything went wrong. I looked at myself in the side view mirror. Frankenstein's monster.

Chapter 9

A few weeks later and I head to Chelsea's house. A couple of my friends live there, and it's the designated meet up spot, being just off Main Street. I bring a six pack. It turns into a party, as it often does. Maybe twelve of us in and outside the apartment. I'm on my fourth beer when my husband shows up. I get up to leave.

"Where are you going?" He asks.

"Anywhere but here."

"Come on Maggie, talk to me."

"I have nothing to say to you." I push my way past him and out onto the balcony overlooking the parking lot.

He walks up behind me. "You're my wife, you can't just ignore me."

I rip off my wedding ring and toss it out between the cars. "I'm not your anything. Leave me alone."

"Jesus, Maggie, what the fuck?" He runs down the steps and starts looking for the ring.

Tears are running down my face and I don't know why.

"Don't worry, we'll find it in the morning when everyone's gone to work." Chelsea says, steering me back inside the house.

"I don't want it. I don't want any of this."

Someone finds the ring in the morning. I stick it in my pocket, but I skip work anyway. I'm hung over and sad and angry. I cried all night, and I don't want this life. I want to trade it in for a new one.

I get fired, of course.

I meet a couple of punk rock looking kids on Main Street who seem to know me. They have a guitar and are playing the Violent Femmes' "Blister in The Sun". I sit down and sing with them for hours. They give me a fiver at the end of the day, and I take it to Beans.

"One mint chocolate hot chocolate, please."

My next job is cleaning rooms at a hotel. They don't care how crazy my hair is as long as I show up and get my rooms done.

I don't have to deal with customers except to give them clean towels. It's a perfect fit. I start bringing my Walkman to listen to while I clean. It drowns out the noise in my head. It is getting loud in there again, but I'm handling it. I start at eight and am done by two each day.

One Friday we get snowed in at the hotel. Anyone who has work the next day can have a free room. I share a jacuzzi room with another housekeeper, Megan. We walk to the gas station down the road and buy cheap beer, then head down to the hotel club to join in the karaoke. I sing *Rainy Day Woman # 12 & 35*. The crowd roars along with me and it feels amazing. Megan and I head back to the room and drink all our beer and watch trashy TV while we soak in the jacuzzi.

Winter passes as I throw myself into my work. The internal voices are back, but I just ignore them as best I can and deal with the constant dull murmur while cleaning rooms and restocking the cleaning carts. The many splintered pieces of myself feel like they've been glued haphazardly back together. It is ugly and messy and imperfect, but it basically works.

My husband tries it on less and less. Most days I can almost forget he exists. I wonder if this is what passes for happiness.

Chapter 10

Summer comes and Sal and I and most of our friends get tickets for an outdoor concert. Bob Dylan headlining and Ani DiFranco opening. I'm practically frothing at the mouth with excitement. Ben and Josh ride in the backseat of Sal's car, everyone singing and laughing and looking forward to an amazing day. Ben is a friend of mine who I am dancing around flirtatiousness with. He is sweet and I think he would date me, but he's not making a move. Josh is younger and likes to be called Moonbeam. I refuse to call him that. He rubs me up the wrong way sometimes, but he is younger, so I try to ignore it.

When we get to the field, Josh and I immediately buy acid off a friendly hippie looking guy, Dave. We chat with him for a few minutes, then find the spot where Sal and Ben are laying down the blanket. I sit with Ben and watch the field as it fills with people, while Josh wanders around chatting to strangers. Friends stop by to chat and then wander back over to their blankets. The field looks like a giant patchwork quilt, full of people.

Josh runs up, "Maggie, I want you to meet someone!"

I'm peaking but the music hasn't started yet so I figure why not?

"Okay."

Josh drags me through a sea of people. "Maggie, this is Victor."

Victor looks like he is in his mid to late 30's. Bald head,

stubble faced and smiling. He smells of roll ups and weed.

"Hey," Victor smiled, "I've never slept with a 'Maggie' before."

I look around but Josh has already disappeared.

"Well, today is not the day." I run away.

I push through the crowd, desperately searching for Sal and Ben... faces looming all around. *Do not lose it, Maggie.*

Ani DiFranco has finally taken the stage and is singing. "Fuck you, and your untouchable face..."

Keep it together, kid.

"Hey, Maggie, you okay? How's that hit treating you?" It's Dave the hippie.

"Hey, Dave man. I can't find my friends, have you seen them?"

"Oh yeah, I was just talking to them, come on, I'll take you over. Good shit, isn't it?"

"Yeah, good shit." Dave leads me back to Sal and Ben. "Thanks, Dave" I fall on the blanket in a heap of relief, heart pounding in my ears.

Ben brushes my hair out of my face. "You okay?"

"I'm going to kill Josh, that little fucker. He left me with some pervert."

Strangle him, beat him till your fists bleed.

I stare up at the sky and let the music wash over me. Ben lays next to me.

"It's okay, you're here now." The clouds look as angry as I feel. They loop and swirl as the sky turns red. I sit up.

"This acid is really good shit."

Chapter 11

A few weeks later I am sitting on my parent's deck with Hannah when the call comes.

"I've got the papers if you want to come sign them."

Divorce papers. Finally.

"Do you want me to come with you?" Hannah asks.

"Yeah, come with. I don't want to be alone with him." I smile. It's actually fucking happening.

My mom drives us to his house. This ride I've taken so many times over the years. This ride will be the last. We pull up in front of his mother's house, which looks exactly as it always has. I am shaking. Hannah and I get out of the car and walk up to the door. He opens it before I can knock.

"Oh, hi, Hannah. Didn't expect to see you. Come on in." Some girl I've never seen is sitting on the couch. At least this one appears to be over eighteen. "Do you guys want a drink?"

"We're not staying." I search the room. "Where are the papers?"

"Hold on a second, I'll go get them." He leaves the room.

I stare at the TV. Wrestling is on. The whole house feels like a tomb to me. A relic, a haunted place full of the ghosts of my pain. I have no desire to waste time in this place. Why is he acting so friendly? The girl? Is this him showing her how he's nice and reasonable and I'm a crazy bitch? Cool. Whatever. Everyone deserves a fresh start, right?

"Here they are. It's a no-fault divorce. We both keep our own stuff and that's it. You sign here," he points to a line on the page, "and fill this paper out if you want to change your name back. That's it."

I fill in the form and sign the page.

"Great, now what?"

"My lawyer files it and we wait for a judge to sign it. Then we'll each get a copy in the mail."

"Brilliant." I hand him his pen back. "Have a good life." I turn and head for the door, Hannah following closely behind.

"Hey Maggie, wait a sec!" He runs up and hugs me. I go stiff in his hands. He lets go and I feel the weight of a thousand worlds lift from my shoulders.

"Bye, Hannah, nice seeing you!" He calls as we get into the car and my mother pulls out of the driveway.

I turn up the radio and open my window. I let the fresh feeling of freedom blow through my hair and I howl out the window with delight.

Chapter 12

I'm sitting outside Beans with yet another hot chocolate when a tall boy with sandy light brown hair asks if he can sit with me. I push the chair out with my foot.

"Sit."

"Chair," he answered. Sitting down.

"Table."

We play a word association game for a few minutes before we start laughing and introduce ourselves. His name is Mark, and he has blue green eyes. We talk for hours. It's easy and light and we connect. He does construction. We go back to Sal's house and listen to music and play Super Nintendo games. When he leaves, I give him my number. Ever the optimist.

He shows up again the next day, and every day for two weeks straight. I show him my poems, we fuck around on Sal's couch (Sorry, Sal). I'm honestly smitten. I write poems about him.

Three days pass without a word. No phone call and he doesn't show up. On the fourth day he comes knocking and I scream through the door. He says he's been working 8 miles away, sleeping in a friend's truck with no change for a pay phone. I tell him to fuck off and forget he met me.

I don't care if any of it is true. The fact that I am so heartbroken is too much. I'm not ready to feel this way. Maybe I'm just in love with the idea of love. Maybe I just can't risk feeling this destroyed again so soon. After an hour of beggingat the door he finally gives up and leaves. I never see him again. But I hear from a girl he is friends with a year later that I broke his heart.

I spend time with friends and try to avoid both boys and alone time. I am successful at neither. But the busier I stay, the less I notice the incessant clamor in my head. The voices come and go, clamoring for attention. Not acknowledging them is difficult, but it's the only defense I've got. I fill my nights with wine jugs and skinny dipping but feel the specter of psychosis hanging over me all the while I know I really can't smoke pot. It's a psychosis trigger, according to my shrink and I need to stop. Still I cling onto the idea that the occasional joint won't hurt. That a bowl once in a while will be perfectly fine. And every time I take a drag, or a bong hit, I lose a little bit more of my grip on reality. Eventually I will get to the point that the sensation of getting high will give me an immediate panic attack. My brain, afraid of madness, will hurtle towards it inexorably in some crazed attempt to get me to just stop. But for now, it's just another layer of the voices, like turning the volume up a notch, or sinking just a few inches deeper into quicksand.

The real truth is that life has gotten stale again. I crave meaning, a direction. Something more important than partying and hook ups. I'm tired of life happening to me, I want to live it on my own terms and leave my imprint behind on something.

Everyone my age is graduating college and choosing a career and living a life, and here I am drinking wine in the woods and hoping to be hit with the inspiration stick. There's no money in poetry. Housekeeping is fine for the moment, but it's not really a career with a future in it. I can't drive, I have no savings, no education, and no real ambitions. The truth is I'm a romantic, with all the aspirations to a life of truth and beauty, but no concrete solid goals or skills.

And what if you never do have any direction? Then what, Maggie?

I meet a boy while skinny dipping at Mia's birthday party. It's a costume party (I'm dressed as Tank Girl), and we're all dancing and drinking and having fun. His name is Jason, and he has gray eyes and blond hair. He's the only one I don't already know, and he keeps smiling at me. When it gets dark and we decide to go skinny dipping, I swim out to the far side of the river. Jason follows me and we kiss and grapple hungrily in the water. I see fireworks behind my closed eyes.

He's away at college, so we mostly talk on the phone. We have little in common. He thinks I do too many drugs, and drink too much. He keeps saying things like, "Be careful." I need to hear it but don't want to. I'm never careful. I wouldn't even know where to begin.

Eventually we decide we're better off as friends. There are too many differences, and we never see each other. I do not need another relationship that is purely based on the physical. That worked out *so* well for me last time.

Chapter 13

I last six months working at the hotel and get a twenty-five cent raise for it. I celebrate by buying some comic books and CDs, then heading over to Beans to read them over a hot chocolate. Twenty-five cents isn't a lot, but it's the first raise I've ever gotten. Definitely worth celebrating.

I'm on my last room of the day when it happens. I lose time. I'm cleaning a toilet and the voices start chatting and then suddenly I'm holding a vacuum and it's running, and I don't know how long I've been standing there. I am angry. Why is this happening again? I need air and time to process this. Acknowledging that my mind is unreliable can be difficult at times, especially when I feel like I've finally got a handle on things. I have invested so much in the idea that I am okay now. I don't know how to handle the possibility that I will always be subject to psychosis.

I put the cart away and I leave. I don't call for a ride or anything, I just start walking towards home, even though it's a twenty-minute drive from work. I walk for over an hour before I hear Alexandra's voice yelling at me from a parking lot.

"What the fuck are you doing?"

"I... I finished work. I was walking."

"You were walking back to town? Along six-eleven? Jesus, Maggie, get in the car."

Alex drives me to her house. I help her unload the groceries and then we head to her room, and she shuts the door.

"Are you okay? Why didn't you call someone for a ride?"

"I don't know. Things got weird at work, and I just decided to walk."

"Maggie, where are you even going? It's ten miles to town. What do you mean, 'things got weird'?"

I tell Alex everything. The voices I've been ignoring, the lost time at work. She sighs.

"Do you want to call your mom? Maybe you should go back to the shrink. You don't want to wind up in the hospital again."

No, I don't want to wind up in the hospital again. I'm not ready to give up, though, and going to a shrink feels decidedly like admitting defeat. I'll give up pot. Maybe that'll sort me out.

Chapter 14

It was a couple of weeks later when the laundromat Sal lives above caught on fire. I'm at Beans (of course) when Sal pulls up in his mustang with his cat in the front seat and Sal his belongings piled in the backseat. I'd heard the sirens but had no idea just how close the fire was. Sal was going to Jersey to stay with his parents. I'd need to find another place to stay tonight, or a ride home.

I crash on Chelsea's couch and catch a ride home from my mom in the morning. The idea of never going back to Sal's hits me like a brick wall. He's definitely going to need a new apartment. All his furniture is smoke damaged. It's like a chapter of my life is ending in the way my relationships tend to: Up in flames.

Back at home, I lay in bed and listen to the voices. I notice they each have colors that flash through my mind when they're speaking. I can hear the different colors and they definitely each have a different agenda and personality.

Paying attention now, are we? Red asks.

I roll over and try to list them all. Blue is always male, and authoritative. Big sky daddy. Haha. Red is of indeterminate gender and full of sarcasm. Like a genderless devil's advocate. Violet is female, and sometimes borders on kind, but feels vain, somehow. She seems to be some kind of evolution of Intuition. Grass Green is male, and reminiscent of the ex, or maybe just some imagined amalgamation of male. Like, all the boys

I've ever loved mixed together. Brown is female, and with a total mom vibe. Some hippie mother Earth kind of thing going on there. Yellow is some weird kind of blonde stereotype, just dumb and slutty. I identify with her most; she's just looking to have fun. I don't know what the colors mean, but they are distinctly different voices, and they all want something different from me.

Maybe it really is time to go back to the psychiatrist.

I stick to work and home for a few weeks, and the occasional late-night coffee at the diner with friends. I stay away from pot and even alcohol. I'm consumed with the mystery of the voices. It doesn't occur to me that this preoccupation is unhealthy in and of itself. An obsession, even.

It feels like a mysterious code to be cracked. Once I understand it, things will fall into place.

That is of course, the dream. The endgame. For things to make sense. For life and my mind to make some kind of logical sense. Then I can stop chasing my own tail and just live. Does anyone really understand what's going on? Is life really just one big cosmic joke that everyone else gets the punchline to?

I put on The Donnas' *Get Skintight* and sing along. It feels dangerous to pay too much attention to the lyrics, they will suck me into a world of delusion if I let them, but singing along is Violet and Yellow's favorite thing to do. Is it dangerous to read too deeply into a song? Probably it is when your head is a minefield of delusions. But this record is straightforward enough to feel safe.

Like you've ever been safe. Red smirked.

She's depressed again. Violet added.

I give up on perfect sobriety and grab a beer from the fridge. Drown the voices. One beer won't hurt.

Chapter 15

I sleep, and dream I am jumping, then bouncing. Higher and higher until I bounce over houses and treetops. I stick out my arms and they're suddenly wings. The wings are feathery, purple and silver, and I fly through the inky night sky. My heart sticks in my throat as it pounds like it's about to burst through my chest. My stomach flips. I go higher. The houses and cars shrink beneath me as I touch the clouds. Now the fear. How do I get back down?

With a crash?

I wake but the fear sticks with me. My life has *always* been full of fear. Fear of disappointing my parents. Fear of going mad again. Fear of being alone, and fear of committing to anyone. Fear of the dark. Fear of creeping things coming out of the shadows. Fear of doors. Fear of mirrors. Fear of failing and looking stupid. Fear of being labeled a fake. Fear upon fear upon fear.

I go sit by the lake and look out at all the trees. The leaves are changing, the greens going yellow, and orange and red. Autumn is the only time I really enjoy being in the Poconos. It's breathtakingly beautiful when you stop to appreciate it.

But soon winter would come with its biting cold and its feet of snow. I do not want to be trapped in this boring town for yet another winter, but it seems inevitable. It's too quiet, too secluded.

It's enough to drive a sane person mad, let alone me. I want to be somewhere with a pulse. With life after 6 pm. With people on the streets and things to do besides get high. Not these sleepy little villages strung together by lengths of empty tree-lined highways and curvy back roads full of blind turns and drunk drivers.

I tried, once, to get my driver's license. I failed miserably, but it was a relief more than a let down. I can't trust my own mind at the best of times, how could I trust it behind the wheel of a one-ton death machine? Yes, a license and a car would mean the ability to leave this place on my own terms, but it isn't worth the stress. Just one more reason why I belong in a city. Someplace with good public transport and things to do.

Public transport might be the answer. Maybe I get a Greyhound bus out of this shithole and head somewhere else. *Anywhere* else. When I was a kid growing up in Jersey, I always thought I'd move to NYC. But New York is expensive, and I have no marketable skills.

Besides, I'm sick of the cold. I want to go somewhere warm. Beaches and swimming pools and palm trees. Cali is far away, and not exactly cheap either. Florida is a bit nearer. It's warm and I have friends and family down that way. I wonder how long I'd have to save up?

At least a year, probably 2 at your wages, says Blue.

Two more winters, two more winters! Red laughs.

Assuming she can keep her head and stay out of the hospital, that is green, injecting his two cents.

Sigh.

I decide to distract myself with religious studies. First up I begin reading everything I can find by Anton LaVey. It's fun, in its way, but not anything I can take very seriously. One too many weird 'how to become a werewolf' essays and screeds about not bathing and I have to bail. I move on to Buddhism and become a bit enthralled. I start with The Way Of The Bodhisattva, then move on to the Dalai Lama and Thich Nhat Hanh. Soon I'm delving into Zen Buddhism. My mother's work friend brings me back mala beads from

India. I attempt to meditate while the voices chatter. I spend my days thinking on koans.

I find religion fascinating, but it just isn't for me. I can't get serious about it. I was raised Catholic, so a good deal of my hallucinations revolve around demons and hell, even though I'm not a believer. I can't pretend to have any idea of what's going on *now*, what could I possibly know about after? What can anyone? It all just seems like speculation, to me. And I am wary of the sort of speculation that will feed my delusions. I have been lucky enough to be aware that my mind is not right, so I try to avoid falling into any of the cliches. My delusions tend to be more covert and insidious. They tend to focus on the secret inner workings, this way I can remain unaware of them. My delusions need to be hunted down and rooted out. I don't think I'm being controlled by the government or that I'm the messiah or any of that. Not anymore, anyway.

What I like about Buddhism is its focus on the here and now. This is at least useful to me. I can focus on right thought, right speech, right effort, and not on whether or not the person sitting across from me can hear my thoughts if I think them loud enough.

For some reason I agree to hang out with the ex of a girl I casually know. We aren't close friends, but she's nice, and he sounds like a complete asshole. He lives near my mom and is vaguely attractive in a grungy sort of way. I go to his house and hang out with his friends. One of them goes to the toilet and the others take turns pissing in his beer. They laugh when he drinks it. We go out back and they have a cage full of actual pigeons. This guy lets them loose and his friend starts shooting at them. I sneak out around the house and go home while they play murder-the-pigeons. I really need to get out of this town.

Chapter 16

I meet another boy. A friend's brother. He is tall and skinny and likes good music and doesn't tell me to drink less or do more. He introduces me to Nick Cave and the Pixies. We go to his house for a weekend visit, and I do not come home for two weeks. My mother is livid. I quit my job at the hotel over the phone. I apologize profusely. I don't know what I'm doing, but it feels right.

He is unhappy with this place, in the same way I am. We are both filled with nervous energy, desperate for change. He suggests we move to the desert. I agree, and a few months later we pack up a U-Haul and drive for five days, through the deep south in the summer heat. I get a massive sunburn on my right arm, chain smoking the whole road trip.

The desert is good. We move to Flagg, a small city halfway up a mountain. There's a university, there's a culture. A small blue oasis in a big red state, as they say. There are artists and musicians and a thriving pub culture that we slot easily into.

We find jobs. We make friends. We adopt pets. We decide to open up our relationship. It becomes strained. We close it back up. I get pregnant.

The ex decides to call me one day. I'm sitting on my sofa, watching TV and eating. My cell phone rings, and I pick it up, expecting it to be anyone but him.

"Hello?"

"Hello, stranger. How's the desert treating you?"

Time has passed, enough of it that I'm not angry at the sound of his voice, just confused.

"It's okay. I like it here. How are you, and what's the occasion?"

I heard a rumor. Is it true? Are you really pregnant?"

"It is and I am."

"Wow. You know, I always thought you'd come back, and we'd give it one last try. I guess it's too late now."

I stifle a laugh. "It seems a bit late now, yeah. So what are you up to these days?"

"Oh, I'm dating a stripper now. I tried dating a smart girl, and we both know how that turned out, so I thought I'd try dating a pretty one."

I roll my eyes at his attempt at wounding me." Right. Is there anything else you wanted?"

"I've got a box of baby clothes here from my sister. I'm going to take them down to your mom's house so she can send them to you. Good luck, Maggie."

"Yeah, thanks, I guess. Tell your mom I said hello."

I hang up the phone and shake off the thin layer of ick that has settled over my thoughts. He's gone, and now he knows I have no intention of ever going back to him.

M is born small but healthy, on Valentines Day. My whole world revolves around this little person, and I dote on them whole-heartedly. Soon we move outside of town to a little pink trailer in Kapchaw Village.

I am secluded outside of town. None of my friends will make the ten-minute drive to visit the entire time we live there. I still don't drive, and with only one car it hardly makes a difference. The only friend I make is a woman who lives across the road. Her son is M's age, and they play together. She and her husband are super friendly at first, but our friendship falls apart when he drunkenly beats her in the middle of our road one night, and I call the cops. He drives off in his pick up and gets arrested for DUI. I go back to a quiet homebody life, just caring for M.

We get a computer. Suddenly, I am no longer alone in the house. The internet opens up a whole new world to me. My first major discovery is a website called The Silver Safe. It is a repository of declassified government documents, but the biggest draw for me is the forums. All sorts of people from all over the world discussing different theories and ideas. I join in on the discussions and make many friends. This internet life begins to take up more and more of my spare time.

We move into a nice doublewide, three-bedroom. We can only afford this because his mother moves in with us. She is a lovely person, and it's nice to have someone to talk to during the day, but it is still awkward. Our relationship is strained, and I spend more time with his mother than with him.

Eventually I have to concede that things here aren't working out. I can tell we make better friends than lovers. We want different things. I want love and passion and partnership and to raise this baby. I do not know what he wants, but it is different in some fundamental way we cannot bridge. He is closed off and I'll never know him, not really. He parties all night and wakes me up at 5 in the morning crying. I am dragging him into adulthood, kicking and screaming. We hold on as long as we can. We get engaged. I cannot go through with it.

When I leave, I am 6 years older and have a three-year old child with me.

I move back in with my parents. They are now in a different, bigger house in Grimsburg, no longer by the lake. I could walk to Beans, if Beans were still there. It isn't though. What I can do is walk my kid to school. He's still too little for that, but time flies and soon it will matter. I'm now close to all my old friends, but they've all moved on. Grimsburg has become a sort of crypt of the past. I'm a stranger here. I no longer belong.

Chapter 17

Back at home, I get a part time job and work when my mom is around to watch baby M. I start saving up all the money I can. When I'm not working, and M is sleeping, I'm on the computer, chatting with Peter. Peter is a guy I met on the Black Vault. He likes to argue in the religious forum, maybe even troll them a bit. He makes me laugh. He lives in England, is a few years younger than me, and isn't into any of the things I am. He likes golf and football (soccer) and works in programming. I like music, poetry and self-destruction. It's an odd combination, but it's refreshing to talk to someone with completely different interests.

Peter introduces me to a skeptics' website, which *also* has forums. So I get sucked into a whole new corner of the internet. People get into heated debates over the smallest of points. Some of them argue just for the sake of arguing. Some of the conversations are nuanced and interesting. I sit back and read, read, read. I make a lot more new friends.

The foundation which owns the website, the JREF, has yearly gatherings in Las Vegas, and Peter and I decide to attend next year's together. We'll finally get to meet in person and share a room.

The conference takes place in January. I decide to use up my savings on flights. My ex and I trade M back and forth every few months, so I will pick the baby up right after my Vegas trip, and bring him home with me. It will eat into my savings and push back any plans to move away, but meeting Peter seems much more important at this point. Honestly, he's the only thing I can think about. Even the voices are obsessed.

Autumn passes at a snail's pace. Now that I have something to look forward to, time slows to a crawl. My heart and mind are continually 3500 miles away. I just want to get through all the damn holidays and get to January.

What good is a man on the other side of an ocean? Red asks.

I don't answer. I don't answer at all anymore, but especially not about Peter. They don't get to have him. The voices don't get a say in this. There are a thousand reasons why this relationship can't happen, but these voices will not get to be one of them. I've worked too hard to claw my life back from schizophrenia's grip.

Winter finally comes to Grimsburg. I revel in the bitterness to the air, the first falls of snow. Funny how quick our perspectives can change. The cold is now just another step closer to Vegas.

I'm hanging out with Alex again. Sometimes we go months without speaking, but then we're besties again, and it's like minutes have passed, rather than months. I spend all my time off either chatting with Peter or sitting around at Alex's house *talking* about chatting with Peter.

"Just be careful, Maggie. Are you sure you don't want to book a separate room?"

"Fuck no. I want to spend every second with him that I can." I've already had exactly this conversation with my mother. "It's only five days, anyway. If things are somehow horrible, I'll call my mom and get her to move up my flight. I *swear.*"

"You aren't even a little bit worried, are you?"

"Are you kidding?" I laugh, "I'm nervous as hell! What if it's all different? What if I've built this all up in my mind and we hate each other? I'm incredibly worried. But I'm also completely sure that it's going to be magical."

"Well, I hope it is. I hope it's everything you want it to be."

Chapter 18

January comes and I pack my bag for the flight. Five days' worth of clothes, 3 pairs of heels, my makeup bag, tooth and hairbrush, Gameboy, and my stack of journals. I haven't written in my regular journal in ages. I've been writing in notebooks directly to Peter for most of a year now. I've filled up three books and am already a third of the way through the fourth. I promised Peter he could read them all. I've never exposed myself to someone this way. It's both exhilarating and terrifying, in equal measure. I wrap up my phone charger and wedge it in my bag. I'm ready to go.

Alexandra drives me to the airport. I am a bundle of exposed nerves, all foot tapping and forgetting to breathe. We blast the stereo, singing along to the CDs we burned on Alex's computer. We're both sing-yelling "I'm Still Standing" when suddenly, we've arrived at the airport and Alex is pulling into the short stay bay.

"Message me when you get there, have an amazing time!" Alex yells as I pull my luggage from the trunk.

"I will! You and mom. See you when I get back!"

"And don't get married in one of those little Vegas chapels!" Alexandra adds as I walk away, waving one hand as my other pulls my pink suitcase behind me.

The flight is long, five and a half hours long, and I spend almost all of it furiously recording my every thought and feeling in my notebook. I am absolutely giddy with nerves and excitement. My stomach rumbles and flips with every butterfly flutter and bump in the flight path. I put on a movie but cannot concentrate. I pick at the lunch they serve. I order a glass of white wine and watch as the minutes slowly tick past. There was a long wait for me upon landing, another two and a half hours before Peter's flight was due in. I was going to walk over to the international gate to wait for him, then we'd take the shuttle bus to our hotel and check in. I stretch as best I can in my seat and try to imagine what our meeting will be like. Will it be awkward, or more like a homecoming? Most probably, a bit of both.

I get my bag after the flight and take a shuttle to terminal 3, all the way on the other side of the airport. I find the waiting area and camp out directly across from the doors. I pull out my Gameboy and try to play The Powerpuff Girls game, but I can't concentrate and give up after twenty minutes. I people-watch instead. Every so often the doors open, and a new stream of people trickle through. Everyone in the waiting area perks up. Will their loved one be the next through the doors? I watch families reunite with tears of joy. I try to imagine why they've been apart, what are their stories? This girl was away at university in another country. That man was teaching English to school children in Japan. This group was backpacking through Europe. I pick up my journal and begin to write again.

Time flies as I write. Suddenly, he's there, standing before me.

"Maggie?" He asks.

I drop my notebook and stand, not believing this moment has finally come. He takes me in his arms. He's shaking. I realize I am shaking too. We kiss and it seems to last so long I can't breathe anymore, and I finally break the embrace.

"Let's get out of here," I say, taking his hand.

I shove my things in my bag and we run to catch the shuttle bus. It is hot and stuffy and slow, but we go to the back, put our bags on a luggage rack and sit down. We kiss like teenagers, barely coming up for breath. After a while we stop and start to talk. Peter hates flying. His breath tastes of whisky, which he'd been drinking on the flight to calm his nerves.

We're staying at the Stardust, where the meeting is being held. After what seems like hours on the hot, crowded shuttle bus, we arrive at the hotel. We check into our room and unpack our bags, then decide to go explore the casino and find a place to get some dinner.

We walk all over the casino floor, have a drink at the bar and find a rainforest themed restaurant to eat at. The walls are painted with murals of jungle trees and banana leaves. We get tropical drinks as big as our heads, something-something-sunrise. A photographer comes around and takes a picture of the happy couple cuddling together in our booth. Peter buys me a print.

After dinner we head back to our room and tumble into bed. There are speakers we both want to see the next day, but for now there is only us.

Chapter 19

In the morning, we wake in a tangle of arms and legs. Peter jumps in the shower while I run down to a kiosk to get muffins for breakfast. I eat my muffin, then we switch places. An hour later we are down in a conference room ready for the first speaker. The talk is good from the reactions of the crowd, but I am somewhere in the clouds, and my memory holds onto nothing but his scent and the feel of his skin beneath my fingers.

Now, with a few hours to kill, we head out to explore the strip. We walk around Caesar's Palace and watch the roller coaster at New York, New York. We wander all the way down to the Luxor and place some bets. On the walk back I realized bringing nothing but heels was a dire miscalculation. We search high and low for flip flops but in the end, I wind up buying a pair of blue suede moccasins. The same shade of blue as Blue voice. They are soft and buttery from the second I buy them, and I wear them for the rest of the trip.

We wander off the strip and hear a gunshot and then, a few minutes later a siren. It is the gas station where we'd bought bottled water twenty minutes before getting robbed, according to a man we pass on the street. We head back towards the strip.

We stop to watch the pirates outside of Treasure Island enacting some sort of attack. There is shouting and smoke, and the crowd around the ship grows bigger. Then we head back to the Stardust. We sit at the bar, Peter ordering whisky while I have a few rum and cokes. I dance around a bit to Peter's amusement. We meet up with a Black Vault acquaintance and his wife. We're all a little drunk and no one can understand anyone else's accent. He is from the deep south. She is from somewhere, I'm not sure where, but her accent is thick to my drunken ear. I nod and smile and feel lost. They eventually leave to move on to another bar, and we head back to the room before we're too drunk to find it.

Morning.

It's time to watch Murray Gell-Mann speak. I bring my copy of The Quark and the Jaguar, hoping to get his autograph. After his talk we find him standing in the Sallway, chatting with the attendees.

"That's a nice dress." Murray Gell-Mann says, looking me up and down and winking.

"Thank you, Mr. Gell-Man, would you sign my book?" I am beet red and barely able to speak. My brain has gone blank, and I am like the proverbial deer caught in headlights.

"No problem." He signs it and hands it back.

"Thank you so much, I'm such a big fan!" I snatch the book from his hands and spin around, nearly walking into Peter in my haste to get away. My heart is pounding and I'm still eight different shades of crimson.

"Did Murray Gell-Man just try to flirt with me?" I whisper as we get into the elevator.

Peter laughs, "He definitely did. You looked like you were going to cry."

"I almost did!" I giggle and feel my face turn some shade of red. "I've just been flirted with by a Nobel Prize winner!"

On the Vegas Strip, day and night have very little meaning. Peter and I find ourselves sleeping in the middle of the day and having meals at 3 am. The five days pass too quickly, and now it's time to go our separate ways. We pack our bags with a quiet sadness, and check out of the Stardust, catching the shuttle to the airport.

Peter's flight is first, so we head to international departures and hang out on a bench outside until he has to leave. I take pictures until I run out of film. We kiss and I cry, and Peter swears to come back as soon as he can. When he leaves, I watch until the doors shut behind him and he's swallowed in a sea of people. These were the best five days of my entire life, and now my heart feels as if it's been ripped from my chest, still beating. With over an hour left until I can check into my flight, I buy a pack of cigarettes and chain-smoke until I feel sick.

Five days without a smoke and look at you. Violet chided.

Fuck off. I think back.

What if this is it and I never see him again? He's my person. I can't let him go so soon. I stub out cigarette number three. I cannot believe that he doesn't feel what I feel. This can't possibly be over.

I spend the entire flight journaling and crying. I am crying when I pick up M and crying when we board our next flight. I try to keep it in check, but the tears slide relentlessly down my cheeks. Thankfully M seems too preoccupied to notice.

I realize that I am lost to this man, I am totally and irrevocably his, and I do not know how I can survive without him.

The next day at work, the voices are especially active. Peter messages as soon as he gets home, he is planning out another trip in March, but the voices latch onto a weakness and are loath to let go.

He HATES you; you are so clingy. One day you will wake up and he'll have changed all his online accounts and you will never hear from him again. Violet was being vicious.

Everyone at work wants to hear about my trip. I keep the details PG and stick to the sights and the conference. I do not want to share my happiness, expose it to the cold, hungry world. This is just for me, and I protect it faithfully.

Chapter 20

Six weeks plod by. Winter is once again the enemy, cold and barren and unforgiving. I play games with M, work evenings and weekends. The voices lie their angry, paranoid lies and I pretend not to hear them. Eventually they start to recede, fading away until their rumblings become unintelligible music. Just rhythms in the back of my mind. I cherish this quiet.

Birds are chirping and the early spring flowers are beginning to bloom when we drive down to the airport to meet Peter. My parents drive, and when we get to the airport, we sit and wait. M climbs the seats beside me as I tap out my nerves with one foot, a morse code of longing and fear. I won't feel right again until I see him.

And then he is there, walking through the doors and looking around. I jump up and he spots us. We run to each other and embrace again. Now my world feels right, a crescendo of emotion falls on me and I hold him tighter.

The airline has lost his bag. We're back and forth with them for an hour before realizing it was the lone bag at baggage claim. He'd borrowed one of his parent's bags and forgotten what color it was. My parents gently tease him the whole drive back to our house. M eyes him up distrustfully. I am simply full of love and relief. I breathe out and it feels like I've been holding onto that breath since Vegas.

In the ten days he stays, I live a whole lifetime. M ignores him for days, except to pour shampoo in his mouthwash. When he finally climbs up onto Peter's lap, seeming to concede friendship, he is covertly covered in poo, which winds up all over Peter and his shirt. Peter laughs it off, and I take M off to the bathroom for a scrub.

We make our plans. He applies for a visa so that next time he comes over, it will be for six months. The wait doesn't seem so bad this time now that we have a plan. I call up an old friend, a tattoo artist, and I make an appointment.

My first tattoo is Peter's name near my hip bone. I tell him I'm doing it, but I'm not sure he believes me until it's done. To me, it's a symbol. I am all in on this.

We get a short-term lease in Florida and set up a home of sorts. We watch the World Cup in various pubs and sleep on a mattress on the floor. Only M has a proper bed. The living room wall leaks and drips every time it rains. We call maintenance, but nothing ever gets done. We lounge around the swimming pool, and I work as a checkout girl in a supermarket. His family come out to visit us. I am nervous, but they are friendly and are wonderful with M.

When his visa finally runs out, we return to England with him.

We stay at his parent's house. It is massive and warm, and I am quickly made to feel at home. We take M to a grotto to see Father Christmas and visit the pub every Sunday with Peter's dad. There is music and cockles and an angry old boy guarding the roast potatoes as if they're coated in gold. We laugh and joke while the old man scowls over his roasties.

After Christmas I take M back to his dad. On my return flight, I am grilled at passport control. The woman on duty questions me relentlessly, trying to get me to incriminate myself in some way. I am just visiting. I am not working; my fiancé is paying for my stay. I am sobbing openly, afraid she will not let me in the country, when she finally sniffs and tells me that I'm doing nothing wrong, but I should be grateful for the position I'm in.

Chapter 21

I love it in Southbend. It's a bustling seaside town and I take to it immediately. When Peter is at work I walk everywhere; the town, the seafront, learning my way around. We go to the cinema almost every week. We go to Southbend United away games whenever we get the chance. His parents take us to London, and to see some castles. We make plans for the future. Before long, I am pregnant with our first child.

Soon my six months are up, and I head back to America while Peter works on getting the right visa to come over and get married. We do everything by the book. There cannot be any mistakes. The stress of having a government able to veto your entire life by withholding a single stamp or piece of paper begins to take its toll on me. Instead of voices, it comes as waves of emotion. I get overwhelmed and cry for hours.

When Peter finally arrives on his visa, we have exactly 90 days to plan and execute our wedding, and then file all the relevant paperwork. I set to work immediately, picking out a venue, buying a dress and suit, rings, and invitations and catering. The list of things that need to be done seems endless.

The day before the wedding I open my dresser drawer to take out the license and put it with everything else we will need for the ceremony. The envelope, which I had placed right on top, is gone. I empty out the entire drawer, piece by piece. It isn't there. My stomach drops and a molten ball of panic forms inside of it. My mother drives me down to the courthouse just as they are getting ready to shut. The tears of a heavily pregnant woman convince them to let us in. Luckily, my mother's neighbor works there, and we get her to make us an official copy. When we get home, we remove the drawer entirely, and find the envelope flat against the back of the dresser. Now we have two copies of the license. Tears of relief slide down my face.

Finally the day arrives. We get married in a little chapel near my parents' house. I am six months pregnant, and the guest list is small. Just close friends and family. Peter's mum and one of his sisters fly out to be there. Alexandra is my maid of honor, and her mother bakes us a wonderful football shaped cake that matches my purple maternity dress. I get the rings confused during the ceremony and get told off by the officiant, but we laugh. It's all perfect.

Afterwards we head back to my parent's house for a reception. There is food and tons of wine from my favorite winery that I can't touch. My mother plays music and dances around. It is November, and bitterly cold, but we stand out on the deck with coffee in our coats and slippers, finally officially legally man and wife. I could cry with relief. Finally something has gone right. My fractured world is just a little more healed and whole.

Our son is born, healthy and squalling, in February. Because nothing can go smoothly for me, I experience peripartum cardiomyopathy, and am back in the hospital when he is four days old. Heart failure. My body is retaining so much water I cannot breathe when I lay down flat. I didn't think to tell anyone, but Peter's mum, a nurse, takes one look at me and knows something is not right. They haul me off, once again, to the emergency room. This time a couple days' worth of diuretics sets me straight. The excess water removed, my heart returns to its normal function. My cardiologist says I am fine, it was a freak thing to happen and there is no reason why we shouldn't have more children in the future.

Soon it is time to leave my parent's house behind and head back to Florida. M's dad has already moved there. Instead of months with no M, we can now have him every other weekend and holidays. It is not perfect, but it is something. It takes me two hours on the bus to get to their house. Baby J and I are always excited to do it, though. We rent an apartment and get our few furnishings out of storage and begin to build a life.

Our first apartment is in a complex with its own golf course. The complex looks beautiful, and the sample apartment is small, but fits our needs easily. We sign and pay our deposit, and are immediately shown to our new home, way back on the other side of the complex. There's a pool nearby, but not as clean as the one up front. There are poorly kept tennis courts with broken nets and graffiti on the side of one of the buildings. The golf course never reopens, and our downstairs neighbors play Duranguense music at all hours, with the bass turned all the way up, shaking our walls. When our lease is up, we move to a new complex a short distance away, and revel in the relative quiet of an upstairs neighbor who likes to vacuum at one am.

Peter's parents move out with one of his sisters. They run a property management business, renting out houses to holiday makers. Soon another one of his sisters joins them. It is nice to have family around us.

J is a happy child, always smiling and dancing his way around wherever we take him. Life itself is idyllic, it feels like one extended holiday. We spend our afternoons by the pool, and our weekends at theme parks and shopping malls. Things like that never seem to last, though, and soon reality cracks the shell of our perfect little world.

Chapter 22

Peter's parents move back home, as there are now too many of them for the business to support. They sell it off and return to the U.K., and we realize we are now in similar circumstances. I have no insurance, and our savings are running low. We make the difficult decision to give up our Florida dreams and return to England. But first we move back in with my parents, to save a bit of money for the trip.

It breaks my heart to leave M behind. The voices savage me, but we have no choice. Financially, there are no other options. In the height of summer we pack up whatever will fit into my mother's minivan, and road trip our way back to Pennsylvania.

Peter likes it there, but to me the very air tastes like failure. Everywhere I turn I am confronted by memories I want to forget. I put my head down and get about the business of making new ones. I don't think anyone understands the way I feel about this place, and it's probably better they don't. Just forget it all and look to the future. I will not miss this place when I leave it.

Before long, it is Christmas time, and M comes to visit with us for a few days. It is magical and heart wrenching in equal measures. I do not know what our futures hold, but I am devastated by the fear in M's eyes. He is trying to be strong, and so am I, but what good does it do anyone?

When M leaves, I cry out entire oceans while I begin to pack. We leave on New Year's Eve.

We move across an ocean with one full sized piece of luggage each. What is left of our belongings jammed into three suitcases. Mostly clothes and some toys and a few books. Everything will need to be replaced. New versions of all our things, with funny three prong plugs and different names. No more pants and sweaters, but trousers and jumpers. I let the past float away on the clouds as we pass over the Atlantic.

At some point over the middle of the ocean, we hit midnight. The air hostesses hand out little plastic glasses of sparkling wine and we all toast and cheer. Happy New Year, new life, new start. I have never put much stock in New Year's Eve, it always seemed arbitrary to me. I don't do resolutions, if I want to change something, I will do it then and there, or not at all. It always feels wrong, counting the new year in the cold crypt of winter. It should all start again in Spring, when life is renewed, if you ask me.

Peter's parents have put a bed in the dining room, so we have a place to sleep while we look for a place of our own. It is not ideal, but it's a room with a door and we try to make the best of it.

Peter cannot sleep. After a few days he sees the doctor and gets sleeping pills. Meanwhile we look for a flat of our own while Peter goes straight back to work. It takes us two weeks, but we find a place and by the third week of January we're moved into our new home.

Our flat is a small two-bedroom, ground floor with doors opening up into the shared garden space. We get a sofa from Peter's boss and a table from his mum's friend, and slowly start building up furnishings. J's birthday rolls around, and his room is soon full of toys. I get him on the waiting list for nursery at the local primary school, and we spend our days watching telly and going to the park and for adventures around town.

Soon the weather warms up and J gets a spot in the morning nursery. It's difficult for me to let him go but he absolutely loves it there. Summer comes and we realize I do not have the right visa for permanent settlement. So J and I get on a plane and travel back to Grimsburg to apply for the correct paperwork in June. We get M to stay with us, and the whole thing takes an entire month to get sorted out. I spend my days filing paperwork and waiting for phone calls while playing with the kids. Our evenings are spent at Alex's house, video chatting with Peter. My spousal visa comes through two days before my scheduled flight back home. The only tears at the airport this time are tears of joy. We are home.

I get my first job working in the kitchen of a local bowls club. I serve and clean and do some prep work. It's only a few hours a week, but it gets me out of the house and gives me some spending money. Before I know it, I'm pregnant. My hours get cut until I'm barely working at all.

Then I begin cramping and bleeding. Peter's mum takes me to the hospital. There is nothing they can do. I spend the night and I am no longer pregnant when I leave. I am crushed, and I cry for the life inside me that never was. After a week of quiet contemplation we go right back to trying, and a month after that we are pregnant again.

Chapter 23

J loves school, and I spend the winter taking him in everyday and slowly but secretly getting larger under my giant winter coat. J makes friends and grows ever more confident. When spring rolls around I dump the coat and am suddenly surrounded by people asking me how far along I am and laughing about how they didn't realize I was pregnant at all.

There are tests upon tests. I get my medical history sent over from America. They monitor my heart, but everything seems fine. My stomach grows big and hard like a fine ripe watermelon. I waddle around blissfully. There is no combination of hormones I react better to than pregnancy hormones. I am forever joyful in pregnancy, one of those annoying women walking around rubbing her belly and smiling beatifically. I am quite sure this will be my last one, so I attempt to really savor the feeling.

I learn about babywearing and decide that I am going to do it. I research different types of wraps and carriers and decide on and purchase a wrap a few weeks before my scheduled cesarean so I can practice using it. I want to be ready when baby C arrives.

C arrives in early July, with dark curly hair, chubby cheeks, and big blue eyes. M and J are both at the hospital to greet her. This time there are no complications, no life-threatening emergencies. All is well and our little family is now complete.

I become one of those crunchy mums. I have a collection of wraps to wear C around town in. I begin using cloth diapers. I subscribe to gentle parenting blogs and become fully immersed in motherhood in a way I never have before. Maybe it's just because I know she will probably be my last, but I throw myself into everything.

C, not to be outdone by J, also begins walking at ten months old. We get her one of those backpack harnesses, and when she isn't riding high on my back, she is running ahead of us on the end of a lead, causing havoc like only a barely toddler can. C is a baby of extremes, either happy and giggling or screaming and crying. She is all chubby cheeks and big blue eyes and far too tiny to be running around the way she does. These are all qualities she will carry with her throughout her childhood.

Chapter 24

The voices are quiet. I almost forget they ever even existed; they are so far from what my life is now. I am in what they call remission, I guess. I don't question it, I just live.

Soon my birthday rolls around, and we plan a night out in London. We will go to a comedy show, spend the night in a hotel, and just be a couple again for a few hours.

The room is small but cozy. A double bed, a telly, and a nice sized bathroom, just a short walk from the theater where the show is being held. We have a wonderful time, and on the walk back to the hotel we make the mistake. Perhaps the biggest mistake I've ever made. We light a spliff.

From the first drag I realize I'm done for. My anxiety skyrockets. My breath catches and I hear a siren and I'm not sure if it's real or not and I look around and think *What have you done Maggie you absolute idiot?!* I pinch it out and we stumble back to our hotel. I try to keep myself calm. *At least get back to the room, Mags.*

We get in the room and Peter turns on the telly. I cannot sit still; I'm jumping out of my skin and my arms feel like they belong to someone else. I don't know what to do with them. Peter looks terrified. I haven't seen him this concerned since my heart failure. I start to cry. Everything feels irrevocably broken, and I broke it. I run to the bathroom to blow my nose. I lock myself in and try to wee, but I can't. I can't understand why I feel like weeing if I don't need to. I don't understand *anything* and the sobs come in big heaving waves. I don't know how long I sit there, but Peter knocks on the door twice.

I can feel my ancestors sitting over me in judgment. I can see them, staring down with stormy eyes. How dare I squander their gifts and their blessings? I was pulled up from the gutter of insanity and given back a full life, and this is what I do?

My mind keeps going over everything I have now ruined. Our wonderful relationship, our family, my sanity, everything I've worked so hard for. It's gone in a blink. I know I'm having a panic attack, but I also know I'm having a panic attack *because* I'm having a psychotic break, and I feel justified in my panic. The delusions weave themselves in around the panic, and I am powerless to stop them. I feel myself wilt beneath the imagined eyes of everyone I've ever cared about. Somehow, they're all aware.

I finally return to the bed and take in Peter's face, drawn and gray with concern. I lay next to him, wanting to bury my face in his chest and forget everything.

We sleep, eventually. I wake up and cry some more because it's all just as I feared. My mind feels disconnected. All is not as it should be. What I thought would be a cute little bonding experience turned out to be me inviting psychosis back into my life. And I knew better. It is all my fault. How can I ever forgive myself? My sanity lies before me in splinters again.

The train ride home is silent and somber. Peter calls out the First Response team and they come to chat with me. I am terrified that they will lock me up in a hospital, but they are kind. We discuss my history, and they reassure me that I can stay home as I have a good support system and am not a danger to myself or anyone else. They refer me to a psych team so I can get medicated and in the system, and they leave us with numbers to call in case I become in crisis in the meantime. I am just relieved to not be hospitalized.

The fear of hospitalization again is all encompassing. I have children now; I cannot allow myself to be taken from them. The idea that I might be on the verge of that situation shakes me to my core. I promise myself then and there that I will never do anything to risk my sanity again.

Peter takes a few days off work. We get takeaways for dinner, and I give up being vegan, as I can't face cooking. I just let Peter order our dinners and eat whatever is in front of me.

The psych team gives me a prescription for quetiapine. It works wonders for my psychosis, but it also makes it a struggle to move at all. I can barely motivate myself to do anything, other than eat. I gain forty pounds before I know what's happened. The weight I can deal with, but the lack of energy is debilitating. I am the mother of young children. I need to be able to get up and play with them, take them to school and the park, but I can't seem to find the energy to get off the couch at all.

School runs are the worst. I often do them in my pajamas and sunglasses to hide the fact that I've spent the morning crying. One day, on the way back home, I get into an argument with the voices. I stop walking and start arguing with the pink door to someone's garden across the road. I don't know how long I'm standing there, by the time I realize what I'm doing, but the other parents are long gone, and the road is quiet except for the occasional car driving past. I slink back home in tears, desperate to find a way to regain control.

I go to my doctor and demand a meds switch. This works out better for me. I have plenty of energy and the weight gain stops. I become a bit restless, but this is infinitely more acceptable. Slowly I begin to eke out a life again. I start helping out at a soup kitchen once a week. I make plans to go out with friends. Sometimes I catch myself in a delusional thought, medication does not erase the reality that I suffer from psychosis. It's more like the colors fade into the background. I sometimes hear them still, but it is muted and lacks the power to draw my attention away from reality. On days when I am stressed out, or don't get enough sleep, things get louder and harder to handle. But the meds give me a lifeline, and I use it to pull myself up out of the mire of delusional thinking day after day. Eventually, it gets easier.

The worst symptom, the one that pops up even when everything else is good, is the tactile hallucinations. I don't get the standard bugs crawling on skin type of tactile hallucinations. I get phantom pains that come out of nowhere, which my mind always assigns some otherworldly explanation. For instance, I will be laying in bed and feel claws digging into my foot. That is obviously a demon dragging my astral form down into hell. That stabbing pain in my right buttock? Obviously being poked by a pitchfork. Now that I think about it, it's almost always demons, even though I don't believe in hell. Gotta love that Catholic upbringing leaving its mark on your subconscious.

Regardless of the demonic explanations, the pain itself feels very real. It leaves me tossing and turning and squirming in bed, while we try to watch a movie, or I try desperately to sleep. Knowing that the cause of these pains is my own mind doesn't really take away their power. It only convinces me that I am somehow *thinking* incorrectly. If I can just figure out how to make my brain work properly, the pains will go away, and everything will be okay. Or so I tell myself.

The worst part of these episodes usually last about twenty minutes to half an hour. Eventually, the pains ease off, and I drift into a restless sleep. On a really bad day, they happen while I'm sitting on the couch, watching TV, or reading a book. But thankfully that is rare. It never seems to happen when I am up and about, doing things and keeping busy. Distraction has always been my greatest weapon against the positive symptoms.

Sometimes it all gets overwhelming, and I cry and cry until my eyes are raw. It's funny, crying used to make me feel better, but these days it seems like a futile gesture. Sometimes I am crying because the pretty lies my mind makes up are nothing like reality. Sometimes I cry because I don't know which is which. Other times it all just gets to be too much, and I want to go back. Have a do-over. Give me back a completely rational, working mind and I promise I will never do anything to mess it all up again. Mostly, I think, it's just me feeling sorry for myself. Eventually I dry my tears, get out of bed, and just get on with living.

One of my favorite ways to combat the tearful days is to walk. I grab my headphones, download a few podcasts, and just walk aimlessly. Sometimes I'll walk the brook path, which is quiet, and a bit removed from the world and the noise and people, and I will sob while listening to whichever podcast I've chosen that day. Other times I will take to the streets, sometimes going off in a direction I don't usually go and just explore the roads, heading wherever my feet direct me.

I do not have all the answers. Remission comes slowly, but eventually I am reasonably whole again. When it does, it brings a whole host of new questions. What do I do with myself now? The kids are older, in school all day. Maybe it's time to start actively living again.

And I do. Years pass in remission, and I begin to trust in my wellness. We find a new rhythm. I take care of myself in a way I wasn't even capable of before. I listen to my body, I sleep as much as I need to eat when I'm hungry, get out and walk when my body wants to move. All of this sounds simple, but it's so different from how I expected my body to do what it was told for so many years. It never occurred to me to listen to what it needed.

Life is so different and somehow so much better than I ever imagined it could be. These days my mind is quieter. It has been for years. I have my meds to fall back on in times of need. Nothing is perfect, but I am happy and loved and supported. I write my little stories in my spare time. I even work to put out a magazine with other writers. I try not to beat myself up too much about how things could have been and enjoy things how they are.

Maybe my sanity is held together with string and tape and glue. The thing is, if it's held together long enough, it heals itself into something entirely new. Maybe it's not everything you dreamed of, but that doesn't mean it can't be something great.

So I sit here, at my desk, summer sun streaming through the back door and the fan pointed directly at me, blowing the hair back from my face, and think:

We did it, Mags.

We made it home.

Needle and Thread
(Special Thanks)

The author would like to thank, in no particular order:

Lucienne LeBeau, for her friendship, her support, and her keen eye.

w.p. Quigley, for always being ready to jump in and help make a vision into reality, and putting his absolute all into everything he does.

DS Vernon, for his support, friendship, humor, and honesty.

The entire Ascendent Publishing team, for being absolute rockstars.

Jim, for being the one who helps me see, and carries me through my darkest nights.

www.ingramcontent.com/pod-product-compliance
Lightning Source LLC
Chambersburg PA
CBHW030531310726
48979CB00010B/1872/J

* 9 7 8 1 9 6 3 9 7 0 0 8 1 *